No Sweeter Love

OLIVIA MILES

~ Rosewood Press ~

Also by Olivia Miles

Grand Central Publishing/Forever
<u>The Briar Creek Series</u>
Mistletoe on Main Street
A Match Made on Main Street
Hope Springs on Main Street
Love Blooms on Main Street
Christmas Comes to Main Street

Harlequin Special Edition
'Twas the Week Before Christmas
Recipe for Romance

Sweeter in the City Series
Sweeter in the Summer
Sweeter Than Sunshine

ISBN 978-0692710142

NO SWEETER LOVE

Cover design by Go On Write

First Edition: May 2016

No Sweeter Love

Chapter One

The sun was beating through the wide glass doors that opened onto the bustling, tulip lined sidewalk of Chicago's famed Michigan Avenue, casting shadows on the plush pale green carpet and catching the perfectly cut diamonds at just the right angle, making them sparkle until they seemed to come alive in their cases. From somewhere in the background, the sounds of piano music subtly filled the room as well-dressed women admired rings and bracelets from arm's-length perspective and men frowned as they contemplated their purchases. Voices were controlled at just above a whisper, the staff trained in the patient, gentle act of persuasion, the customers all too happy to mull their decisions. It was a pleasing atmosphere, elegant and carefully crafted; a place where wishes were made and dreams came true.

At least, that's what they'd told her when she'd interviewed for the position last week.

Claire Wells smoothed her grey A-line skirt and did her best to relax her face. She didn't need to look in one of the store's many silver-framed mirrors to know that the line between her brows had returned, and that if she didn't find a way to keep it at bay, she'd probably need to invest in some expensive wrinkle-prevention cream with what little remained of her dwindling savings account.

She was thinking too much. Worrying too much. She was feeling sorry for herself again, really, and she'd promised herself she wouldn't do that anymore. After all, things were on the up and up. She had a job, even if it was far less interesting than her previous position at the auction house. Still, it was a step in the right direction. Before long she'd be able to get an apartment of her own again, with a proper bed. She smiled at the thought of her cousin's lumpy couch soon fading into her memory.

Knowing she needed to keep busy in between customers, Claire took the key from her wrist and unlocked the engagement ring display to straighten a case. She tried not to let her eyes linger too long on a particularly exquisite brilliant-cut solitaire set on a pave band, but it was too late. One glance and that was all it took for that pang to hit, hard and often at random, straight in the center of her chest, bitterly reminding her of everything she'd almost had and somehow lost.

She locked the display case quickly and stood, squaring her shoulders as she looked out the glass doors onto the busy street where the crowds were starting to thicken as work let out for the day, and shoppers hurried by, clutching their paper bags by the handles, their eyes shielded by sunglasses. Her feet hurt from hours of standing in heels—she hadn't even dared to take a lunch break. It felt too awkward, too presumptuous this early into her new position. But now her stomach was starting to rumble and her mouth felt a little dry, and her lower back was throbbing from too many nights on that pull-out couch—and her feet! Claire darted her eyes to her boss, an impeccably dressed middle-aged man named Louis, who was busy assisting a white-haired woman with an equally white small fluffy dog tucked into her designer handbag, before reaching a hand down to ease the back of the stiff shoe from her heel. She closed her eyes, sighing in momentary relief, but startled when she heard her name being gently called in a thick, French accent.

"Claire? Could you assist this gentleman, please?" Louis's jaw pulsed as his dark eyes held steady. It wasn't so much a question as a request.

Claire put on her most pleasant smile as she maneuvered her foot back into the stiff shoe, grimacing against the pain, and swept her eyes over the room to search for her next client, finally setting on the man who was walking in her direction, the smile on his lips fading with each step.

Claire blinked as the air seemed to stall in her lungs, and she told herself it couldn't be him—he'd said he'd left—that he had no reason to be back so soon, unless . . .

The alarm in his eyes matched hers, and she could see the roll of his Adam's apple as he strode to the counter. For one pathetic moment she thought maybe he'd sought her out, maybe he'd come here to apologize, but then she remembered that this was only her third day on the job, and she hadn't heard from Matt since he'd broken her heart three months ago.

More like three months, fourteen days, and oh, about seven hours ago.

"Well, this is a surprise," he said tightly.

Claire raised an eyebrow, looking him square in the eye. "It sure is. I thought you'd moved to California." They had a lovely apartment picked out, just a short drive from the beach. She'd planned to paint the walls a pale, dusky blue to match the sea. They were going to be so happy. . . Or so she'd thought.

She tipped her head, determined to maintain a cool façade, even though her heart was beating out of her chest and the air felt thick and warm and she was aware of beads of sweat beginning to collect at her hairline.

"Change of plans." He shrugged, giving nothing else away.

Claire gripped the edge of the counter. "A change of plans?" she repeated, squinting at him. She'd thrown away her life for those plans—quit her fantastic job when she was finally about to get a big promotion, subleased her sunny apartment, sold off her furniture—and he'd had no intention of seeing them through. Not with her. Not at all, it would seem.

"I decided to stay in Chicago after all." His grin was a little sheepish, something Claire would have found either endearing or infuriating under other circumstances, but she couldn't think about that now. All she could think about was the fact that he'd been in town all along, all these months. And he'd never checked in on her. Never called. Never emailed. Never tried to make things right.

"What made you change your mind?" she asked, swallowing hard. It wasn't her. That much was obvious.

Matt crammed his hands into the pockets of his khakis and glanced at the jewelry case, his cheeks turning ruddy. Claire felt her heart sink. Of course, she realized with a start. He'd met someone else. Someone he wanted to be with. Someone worth staying for. He'd made new plans for himself by tossing aside all the ones they'd made together.

From her periphery she caught Louis frowning at her. She lifted her chin and pulled in a deep breath, but it shook when she released it.

"Well, what can I do for you?" she managed.

Matt waited a beat before asking, "Why are you working here?"

Claire gave him an icy smile. He had no clue. No idea of the pain he had caused her, the damage he'd created. The dreams he'd shattered. "I quit my job to move to San Diego," she reminded him.

Tears prickled the back of her eyes and she blinked

quickly. This was supposed to be the first week of the rest of her life—at least that's what her cousin Hailey had said when she blandly accepted the position, her shoulders sinking, before uncorking a chilled bottle of Chardonnay in a vain attempt to celebrate.

The first week of the rest of her life. Her *new* life. The one without Matt in it.

And yet here he was, nevertheless.

"I just assumed you could get it back . . ." He frowned.

She managed not to scowl at him, just in case Louis was still watching. "What can I do for you?" she asked again, clearing her throat to signal that their personal conversation was over.

"I'm just here to pick up something. They called and said it would be ready today."

Claire nodded. Easy enough. They kept all the orders boxed and labeled on the bottom shelf of the purchasing station. She went to search for it without a word, but her legs shook as she crossed the carpeted floor. There were only three boxes ready for pick-up. She wondered what she might have done had she come across the box earlier. His name was right there on top, clearly typed in a clean serif font on a crisp white label. She blinked at the familiar letters, and then gripped the box in her hands. The sooner she handed it off to him, the sooner he'd be gone again. And then she could get back to her new life. Work on forgetting him again.

Only something told her it wouldn't be any easier this time around.

"Here you are," she said, sliding the box across the glass counter.

He reached into his pocket and retrieved his wallet, but she stopped him. They had a strict policy about this type of thing, and she wasn't about to rush the process just to save her humiliation.

"Please take a look at the item and make sure it's to your liking."

He hesitated and set his wallet on the counter. It was the wallet she'd given him for Christmas last year, and she felt both touched and confused that he still used it, until she realized he was practical like that, not sentimental. She was the one who had held on, after all. While he was the one who had moved on.

The wallet was made of fine Italian leather. She'd gone to four different department stores to find just the right one. She had a childish urge to ask for it back.

Shifting her attention from the memory of their last holiday together, Claire eyed the jewelry box instead. His mother's birthday was next month; it wasn't like Matt to be so on top of gift giving, but then what did she know? He was full of secrets, it now seemed.

The box was their standard small size. Most likely earrings, she decided. It was his mother's sixtieth, Claire now remembered. They'd talked about coming back to Chicago for the party . . .

She gritted her teeth, hoping to make a quick, polite comment on his selection and close out this transaction, but her blood felt like it drained from her face when she saw the diamond engagement ring resting primly on its satin pillow.

For a crazy second she thought this was a setup. Some sweeping romantic gesture where he'd get down on one knee, tell her he'd missed her, that he couldn't imagine another day without her. That he'd had a change of heart.

But then she remembered that he *had* had a change of heart. He'd made that clear when he'd broken things off the day the moving trucks arrived to carry what few belongings she hadn't already sold off to her new life—with him—in California.

"You're getting married?" she cried, puncturing the calculated silence of the store.

From the corner of her eye she spotted Louis's stern glance, but she didn't care. Her cheeks were on fire, her chest was pounding, and she felt for a strange moment like she might be sick or fall over.

"I can explain," he said warily.

"We just broke up three months ago!" Now Louis was muttering something to the woman with the poodle, and with a menacing frown, beelining toward her.

"Is everything okay over here?" he asked, his eyes drifting mildly to Matt.

"Everything is fine," Claire said quickly, swallowing hard. She had the panicky feeling she was on the verge of tears.

Louis leaned forward to admire the ring. "Excellent choice, sir. And congratulations." He turned to her, his stare cold. "Ms. Wells." He nodded and brushed past her.

Claire grabbed the slip of paper that was tucked into the box and walked to the far end of the counter to handle the transaction.

Matt slid along the glass counter, his voice eager. "Claire. I can explain. You know I was in a serious relationship before I met you, and . . . the truth is that I was still in love with her."

Still in love with her? Her vision was starting to go in and out. Claire pushed her fingers to her temples and blinked at the computer screen, not even sure she remembered how to use it.

"Claire?" Matt's voice was low, urgent, but her attention was now focused on the screen, on the payment information, and the glaring reality of how much he loved the woman he'd dumped her for. The sum was huge. For some reason this shocked her, even though, somewhere in her rational mind, she knew the value of the items in the store. She remembered the way Matt had balked at the price of the white slip-covered sofa she'd found for their new, West Coast lifestyle.

"I don't think there's anything left for us to discuss," she said, not meeting his eye. She stared at his hands, the same hands that she had held, interlacing with her fingers. They were both rough and smooth. Warm. Familiar. Now someone else was holding them.

Finally, he slid his credit card across the counter. She processed the order and placed the receipt and one of their signature heavy, ballpoint pens next to it, silently urging him to sign. The lump in her throat made it impossible to speak. Besides, what was even left to say?

Matt sighed as he tucked the small box into his pocket. "For what it's worth, I hope things work out for you, Claire."

She pursed her lips together, giving him a cool look. "The way they've worked out so well for you?"

He smiled sadly, and turned from her for the last time. She watched him go until he disappeared into the crowds on the sidewalk. He was wearing the blue pinstripe shirt she'd helped him select last December, at a post-Christmas sale. He probably didn't remember that. Probably didn't care.

But she'd cared. And as the tears sprung to her eyes and a sob sputtered to the surface, she knew with horrible certainty that she still did.

*

Ethan Parker listened patiently as the female voice shouted accusations directly into his ear, the volume rising steadily as emotions charged, and silently pleaded that, unlike the girl he'd disappointed last week, Marla wouldn't dissolve into tears or show up at his office with a surprise invitation to talk. The guys over in the sports department had had a field day with that one, and the middle-aged receptionist would no longer meet his eye.

"You know what you are, don't you?" Marla's voice hissed through the receiver. Without waiting for a response, she said, "A *womanizer.*"

He didn't quite know what to say to that, or if she even wanted him to say anything at all. If experience had taught him anything, it was that Marla was looking to vent, hoping to have the last word, to hurt him the way he had—unintentionally—hurt her.

He kept quiet. There was nothing he could say to Marla that would make her feel any better, not unless he wanted to lie to her, and he didn't lie to women. That was one rule he followed faithfully.

The call ended with a messy clamor followed by a steady dial tone. Ethan sighed and set the phone back on its cradle. He'd received sixteen emails since Marla had called, and the newest one was from his mother, no doubt wanting to check in again about next weekend's family wedding.

He clicked on the email at the bottom of his list instead, hoping to shake the words that continued to echo in his head. A womanizer. It wasn't the first time he'd been called that, and no doubt it wouldn't be the last, but it didn't seem entirely fair, either. He'd made no promises, offered no hope of something lasting or meaningful. He didn't lead girls on; he always made it clear what he was offering. And that was a bit of fun. Nothing more. Certainly nothing less.

And yet it so often ended like this. Tears, accusations, ugly scenes.

He shook his head. He'd been upfront with Marla; this

wasn't his problem.

The email from his mother, however . . . now that was a problem.

He clicked on another email instead, this one from his boss inquiring about the status of his latest article—an inside look at the West Loop's newest gastropub Ethan had visited last weekend with Marla. The food had been fine, but the eager glint in his date's eye, and the endless mention of her best friend's upcoming baby shower, had left him with a bad feeling, and he was struggling to give the place justice. Ethan eyed the handwritten notes he'd jotted on the "L" ride into work this morning and shot back a quick reply: "Just needs a final polish."

More like a revisit. He'd stop by tomorrow, this time alone, or maybe with a friend from work. Thursdays were the start of the weekend for the local social scene; he'd get another perspective, set the alarm early, and write a quick draft.

The article wasn't due until Friday, but Jud knew it wasn't like Ethan to wait until a deadline to deliver. It was all that suggestive talk about babies and settling down. It was the stress from this damn wedding. This email from his mother. The third since yesterday.

He'd have to reply . . . eventually.

Ethan's phone pinged and his hand stilled on his computer mouse. More name-calling from Marla? Or perhaps Celeste from last week still hadn't finished having her say. Or maybe it was his mother, wanting to make sure things went a little smoother on this upcoming visit, wanting to lecture him on discretion and behavior and all those other things he didn't want to hear at his age.

He'd have to respond eventually. It was that or skip the wedding entirely, which he'd love nothing more than to do, except that would make him the worst son, brother, and cousin imaginable, and there was already enough talk about him in the small town of Grey Harbor, Wisconsin, where he'd grown up. And now faithfully avoided.

Bracing himself, he punched in his password and pulled up the screen, grinning when he saw the text from his best friend: Busy tonight?

He checked his watch. It was half past five. The article wasn't due for another two days.

And Claire Wells was one girl he could never say no to. And the one woman in his life he never wanted to avoid.

Chapter Two

Claire stepped out of the cab and dashed across the street, her eyes darting in defense all the way to the door of her favorite bar. She and Matt had never come here together, she reminded herself firmly as she followed a couple inside the well-air-conditioned room. She could stop feeling so nervous and jumpy, stop looking for someone who wasn't there.

This was her safe place. Her and Ethan's place. Where they'd laughed and cried, though mostly laughed. They'd first come here two years ago, when Ethan was writing an article on the River North nightlife scene. With its candlelit tables and warm wood tones, it was both cozy and inviting. It was a special place, considering she had only ever come here with her best friend.

Ethan had promised to arrive early in the hopes of securing a coveted table on the roof deck terrace which opened from May through September. Seeing no sign of him at the big, loud bar, Claire wound her way to the staircase at the back of the room and hurried up them, the warm sun at the top landing promising a pleasant summer evening, but even the thought of a blood orange margarita did little to boost her spirits. Her heart felt heavy as she reached the last step and hovered at the edge of the concrete deck, the Chicago skyline climbing high around her in all directions.

Her eyes swept to the right, and then the left, reflexively searching for Matt. *He's not here*, she scolded herself firmly. *With any luck you'll never see him again.*

She marched forward, looking for tousled brown hair, crinkly hazel eyes, and a smile that made her feel like she was home even though she was nowhere near it and didn't even know where home was anymore.

From her periphery, she caught some movement—Ethan's arm was raised high, gesturing to catch her attention, and her shoulders sank in relief when she caught his eye. There. Everything would be better now. She'd tell him what happened. She'd shed a few tears. By the end of the night, they'd be joking about it. All that heartache would be forgotten, or at least put on pause.

"Have you been waiting long?" she asked, as he stood to meet her and give her a quick hug, their usual greeting.

"Long enough to get another call from Marla," he said wryly, dropping back into his chair. His shirt sleeves were casually rolled and his sunglasses were neatly folded on the table. She eyed his drink—half finished. Possibly not his first.

Claire thought hard. "Remind me again who Marla is." But she knew. Marla was one of many girls that had walked through Ethan's revolving door.

"Marla is the one I met at that charity thing last weekend," he said, reaching for his beer.

"Ah, yes. The kindergarten teacher who took down her online dating profile after you invited her to dinner the next night." She rolled her eyes. Why these women fell for Ethan never ceased to amaze her. Sure, he was cute, with those twinkling eyes and that wide smile, and he certainly knew how to put on the charm, but in the three years she had known him, she had yet to see him get close to any woman. Well, other than herself.

"Tell me," Ethan said, leaning eagerly across the table until Claire could see the faint dusting of freckles across his nose. "How much clearer do I need to be? They all make it sound like I've led them on. I don't lead women on."

Claire picked up her menu and then set it back down. She'd been here enough times that she didn't need to skim for something new. She knew what she liked. What made her happy. On a warm June night, that margarita would be just the trick. She might even have two or three, considering the day she'd had.

Her chest felt tight again just thinking about it.

"You don't lead women on," she confirmed, and Ethan fell back in his chair, casually grabbing his drink on the way, seeming satisfied. "But, you do break a lot of hearts."

He shrugged. "But I never promise anything. If they get their hearts broken, it has nothing to do with me."

"Except maybe it does. You're charming. You make them feel special. You're cute . . .enough." She gave him a cheeky smile. "You know what you're doing. You know what you're getting into with these women."

"A night of fun, maybe more than one night. Sure. But I don't promise them anything," Ethan pointed out, setting his beer back on the table.

No, he didn't. Unlike someone else she knew.

"I ran into Matt today," she blurted. She blinked at Ethan, and was rewarded by the knit of confusion between his eyebrows.

"But—"

"You thought he'd moved? Turns out he's been in Chicago all these months. He never left." Hot tears threatened to spill if she blinked again, and she snatched the napkin, damp from condensation, from under his beer bottle.

"Stop. You need a drink." Ethan signaled to the waitress, who caught one glimpse of his smile and hurried to their table, barely registering Claire's existence. He ordered a blood orange margarita for her without even asking, and another beer for himself. "Okay," he said when they were alone again. "What happened?"

"He came into the store," Claire said, trying to discreetly dab the corners of her eyes. "To buy . . .an *engagement* ring." Just saying the words made her chest ache.

"The bastard," Ethan said, and despite herself, Claire burst out laughing.

"He is a bastard," she agreed, grinning as a tear escaped and wove a path down her cheek. She wiped at it with the back of her hand, as more followed.

Ethan pulled back in his chair and hooked an ankle over his knee. "Seriously, though, Claire, I don't why you should be upset. The guy was a jerk. He left you with no job, no apartment—"

"I know," Claire said, and she did, rationally speaking. The other part of her, however, still longed for him. For the time they'd shared. For the plans they'd made. For the life she thought they would have together.

"But you are upset," Ethan observed. "Why? You're young, pretty; you should be out having fun. Instead, you're sitting here crying on a beautiful summer evening. Although, is it technically spring? It is, I believe."

"It is still spring," Claire agreed. But summer was just a week away. She'd thought by summer she'd be in a better place. With a good job, a great new apartment, maybe even a new boyfriend. Instead, she was still broke, still homeless, and still single.

And still crying over Matt.

"I don't even have a place to live. Hailey was so excited when I got this job. I know she doesn't say it, and I know she's my cousin, but she wants me out of that apartment. It's a one bedroom." A small one bedroom. A one bedroom with two closets to its name, to be exact.

"You could always move in with your dad," Ethan said, and again, Claire laughed.

When her mom had passed away a year and a half ago, her father had surprised everyone by selling the family home and buying a condo in the Florida Keys. When Claire visited him, she'd been surprised to discover that he'd developed a passion for shuffleboard and Bingo night in the retirement village's recreation room. It had pained her at first, but at least she knew her dad wasn't lonely.

She was the lonely one. Not that she'd be worrying her dad with her troubles. "Maybe I'll go visit him," she said pensively. "When I have enough money saved up." Her eyes welled up at that thought and she started crying harder, aware of Ethan's disapproving frown across the table.

"Matt doesn't deserve these tears," he said in that matter-of-fact way of his.

She knew he was right, of course he was right, but when did reason ever have a place when it came to matters of the heart?

"You wouldn't understand," she insisted. As much as they had in common, it ended when it came to their approach to relationships. Whereas she sought them, Ethan avoided them. "I really loved him, Eth. We had plans made. We'd picked out a new home, furniture even." She blew her nose loudly.

"You picked out furniture together." Ethan shook his head. "Do you hear yourself? That's what your forties are for, Claire. Or at least your late-thirties."

"You're in your thirties," she reminded him, drawing attention to their three-year age difference.

"And look at me. I'm on my second beer, I have a great job, a fantastic apartment, and I haven't cried myself to sleep since I was eleven years old and my pet fish died. And my sisters still tease me over that. Why give yourself the aggravation? Why put yourself through it?"

"Because there's more to life than having fun," she told him, her tears finally stopping as her exasperation grew. It wasn't the first time they'd had this conversation, but nothing had changed since the last time they'd discussed it, back when she'd announced she would be moving to San Diego and Ethan had been less excited for her than she'd expected. "Don't you feel empty with all these women floating in and out of your life? Wouldn't you like to truly connect with a woman, share something with them?"

Ethan shrugged. "I connect with you. You're all I need, babe."

Claire tipped her chin, giving him a long, hard stare. "You know what I mean."

The waitress reappeared with their drinks, once again lingering to give Ethan a slow, secret smile and doing a perfunctory job of handing over Claire's cocktail without so much as a glance in her direction.

Ethan emptied his beer into a frosted glass. "The difference between you and me, Claire, is that you take life too seriously."

She poked the ice cubes in her drink with her straw, watching them float around in the glass. Maybe she did take life too seriously. But what was so wrong with that?

"I got fired today," she announced, and even though she'd told herself she hated that job, and even though she knew it was just a temporary thing anyway, her chin began to wobble just a bit.

Ethan's expression immediately creased with concern. "What? Why? Wait. Don't tell me it was because of —"

She closed her eyes. "I couldn't help it. I got emotional. I tried to explain to Louis, but it seems that it being only my third day of work and all, I was still in the probationary period." She shook her head. "I let that guy ruin my life *twice*."

Ethan cocked an eyebrow. "I was afraid to say it, but yeah, you did."

If they'd been sitting side by side, she would have swatted him for that comment, but instead, Claire buried her face in her hands. For a moment, the world went dark, and all there was were the sounds of voices, traffic two stories below, laughter from the table behind her. She dropped her hands and reached for her drink and took a long draw on the straw. She'd have to get a job, and soon. But she couldn't worry about that tonight. It would defeat the point of coming here. She'd worry about it tomorrow. Lord knew she had time to do it.

"I don't know what I'm going to do," she muttered.

"I know what you're going to do." A gleam had appeared in Ethan's gaze. "Come to my cousin's wedding with me. Next weekend. I need a date and you need a break."

Claire brightened a bit. A break did sound nice . . .and she did love weddings. She had that lavender silk dress that she never had a chance to wear. "Where is it?"

"Door County," he replied, referring to the lakeside resort town a few hours north of the city. "Grey Harbor, where I grew up. We'll ride bikes on the beach, eat good food, get a little drunk. By the time we get back to the city, you won't even remember who Matt is."

Claire wasn't so sure about that, but she did like the sounds of it, and it wasn't like she had anything better to do.

"You're sure you don't want to bring a proper date?" she clarified. Ethan liked to have a good time, and she certainly wasn't going to be entertaining him in that sense.

Ethan looked at her like she was half-crazy. "To a family event? No. Definitely no."

Claire smiled for the first time all day. "Just checking." She shrugged, seeing no reason to pass up such an attractive offer. "All right. I'm in."

*

By the time she'd pecked Ethan on the cheek and they'd each hailed cabs travelling in opposite directions, Claire was feeling almost completely better. She settled herself against the leather seatback, wrinkling her nose at the overwhelming scent of pine air-freshener, and rolled down the window to bask in the glow that always followed a night out with Ethan.

"Where to, miss?" The cabbie's brow arched in question in the rearview mirror, and, without thinking, Claire rattled off her address.

Her *old* address. The one she'd lived in before her world had been ripped out from under her. Or maybe until she'd thrown it all away. For a man. And a very undeserving one at that.

All at once, her good mood was spoiled, and the heavy weight of today's events came rushing back, thudding in her gut and causing her breath to catch just a little.

"I mean, no. Lincoln Park, please," she said, stammering on her words as she gave her cousin's address instead. An address she may as well get used to, seeing as she wouldn't be in a position to move out anytime soon now. Not unless another job came along. And she'd been lucky to find this one.

Claire leaned her head back and watched as the city whizzed by her. The air rushed against her face, cooling her cheeks, erasing the tipsy buzz she'd left the bar with and replacing it with muddled thoughts and murky memories of a day gone bad.

At the next red light, Claire searched the crowds for Matt's face—something she hadn't done in months, and now would have to break herself from doing, just like she'd had to force herself to stop staring at the pictures she'd kept from happier times. Hiking trips. Biking trips. Lazy Sundays on the beach.

She closed her eyes tight, but it was no use, his face was there, clearer than ever. She wondered if he'd proposed tonight. Or if he'd slipped the ring into his sock drawer instead, set aside for the weekend, or maybe a special occasion. She wondered if he had a plan. Something cheesy but still so romantic. She wondered if he'd ever planned on proposing to her.

"Miss? Miss?"

These thoughts were still swimming through her mind when she opened her eyes to see the cabbie frowning at her, the meter stopped, the engine a soft purr over the talk radio.

"Oh." She fumbled through her handbag for her wallet and handed over a crisp bill, not bothering to ask for change, even though she'd overpaid. She just needed to get out of the car, upstairs, and into her bed.

But then, she no longer had a bed. She'd sold it to that cute red-haired girl who had just graduated from college, her life ahead of her, her eyes full of hope.

Her shoulders felt weary as she fished out her key and began the climb up the brownstone steps. She gritted her teeth, wondering how she would break the news, or if she could hold off for a few more days, maybe until she found another job.

Hailey was sitting on the couch in the living room watching television when Claire pushed open the door. When she spotted her, Hailey guiltily dropped her feet from the coffee table and stood up.

Claire kicked off her shoes, vowing to never wear them again, or at least not until they were properly vetted, and wondered idly if Louis would take her back if she begged him. Or bribed him. He had a thing for pocket squares, she'd noticed. And small dogs.

Her shoulders sank. It was no use.

"Don't worry," Claire said, waving away her cousin's concern. "I'm not ready for bed yet." Just the thought of more months on that pull out made her lower back spasm.

Hailey hesitated, and then slowly resumed her spot on the couch. "I have to get to sleep soon anyway. I'm opening at the café tomorrow," she explained. "There's only ten minutes left to this show and I'm hooked. Have you seen this one before? These people are double agents, and—Oh! It's back on."

Claire felt uneasy, like a sudden charity case. Hailey was kind, and she claimed she was happy to give her a place to crash for as long as she needed one, but there no was no denying the twinkle that had caught her eye when just that morning—Imagine!—Claire had mentioned she'd be looking at apartments that weekend.

Claire groaned to herself. She'd have to cancel those appointments now. And the one had looked so promising from the photos—an iron balcony and everything! She'd imagined flower pots, and a little bistro table, and inviting Hailey and their friends Lila and Mary over for iced tea or wine . . . Now she'd be lucky to have a place before fall.

She'd just have to ask Hailey if she could grab a few hours at the Corner Beanery again. Or maybe she'd see if Lila needed any administrative help at her advertising agency. Claire chewed her thumbnail. Last time she'd asked, Lila had winced and explained that they were fully staffed, but that she'd keep Claire in mind, of course. And Mary's ice cream parlor was also complete. So, the café it was then. The thought depressed her. Even though she worked hard, she couldn't help feeling that really, it should be her paying Hailey, not the other way around.

Claire stayed quiet as she padded across the room barefoot and sunk into the armchair near the window. She watched the last few minutes of the show impassively, understanding little and absorbing even less. When the credits finally rolled and Hailey gave a satisfied sigh, she took a big breath and announced, "I saw Matt today."

Hailey's eyes sprung open, her attention now fully pulled from the glowing screen. "You what? But, I thought he'd moved to California!"

Claire's smile was grim. "Turns out he's been here the entire time. Never left."

Hailey blinked. "I'm confused. Where did you see him? What did he say? Are you okay?"

There was so much to discuss and so much she didn't want to share, as much as she needed to say it, to have it out. She and Hailey told each other everything—always had, since they were five years old and their parents moved them into the same school district so that as only children they'd have family.

"I saw him at work. He was picking out a ring. He's getting married. To a girl in Chicago. His ex, actually. I barely remember him ever mentioning her, yet it seems that he was always in love with her. And no, I'm not okay." Her voice cracked, and before she could even start to cry, Hailey had leapt from the couch to wrap an arm over her shoulder.

"It's going to be okay," her cousin soothed, stroking her hair the way they'd done when they were little. The way she'd done when Claire's mom had died. When Matt had left. It had brought more comfort to Claire than she'd known at the time, but looking back, she always shuddered to think what she might have done had she not had her cousin.

She'll understand, Claire told herself firmly. Hailey understood everything. They'd known each other all their lives; they'd been raised more like sisters than cousins.

Hailey knew every detail of her life, every emotion, every heartache; every small memory . . . it was all shared.

She turned, ready to tell her cousin the worst of the day's events, but the concern in Hailey's eyes stopped her. She bit her lip instead, looked away, brushing her hair back from her face to fiddle with her earring.

Guilt gnawed at her. She had to tell her the truth, but to do so . . .

Not tonight, she decided, not until she'd figured things out. She'd come up with a plan. She'd spend all day tomorrow pounding the pavement for a new job. She might even ask Louis to take her back—what could it hurt? There had to be a match for her experience somewhere. She just hadn't found it yet. Perhaps tomorrow would be the day!

She'd try everything, and only once she knew it was hopeless would she tell Hailey the truth. That she had messed up, that her life was in shambles, and that the coat closet would remain filled of all her worldly possessions for at least another few months. And hopefully not more.

"Ethan invited me to a family wedding next weekend," Claire said, happy to move onto another subject. "We'll leave next Wednesday. I guess it's a big to-do. Lots of parties before the big event."

But Hailey frowned. "Your boss is already willing to give you time off?"

Claire felt her cheeks flame. "Oh. Well, he's still working out my shifts," she said. "It's not going to be a regular nine to five schedule."

To her relief, Hailey just shrugged. "Well, if you need to pick up some extra shifts at the café, just let me know."

"Thanks," Claire, said. "That sounds great."

Because it did sound great. And because thanks to Ethan and Hailey, she had almost stopped thinking about Matt and that engagement ring, and the fact that the entire time she'd loved him, he'd loved someone else.

Chapter Three

Even though the Corner Beanery didn't open for another hour, Claire was happy to arrive early, before the commotion that always came with the turn of the sign as busy commuters popped in for coffee on their way to the "L" station just a few blocks down the street.

"Need any help?" she asked as Hailey walked around the small room, flicking on the lights.

"On your day off? Sit. Relax. Something tells me you aren't going to get much of that once Ethan picks you up today."

Claire settled into a coveted table near the window, normally occupied from morning to night. "Actually, I think it will be very relaxing. Ethan said we'd ride bikes—"

"Bikes?" Hailey started to laugh as she poured the

coffee beans into the grinder. "Somehow I struggle to picture Ethan on a bike."

Claire wrinkled her nose. The image she pulled to mind was awkward, or at least, not exactly typical of Ethan's fast-paced lifestyle. Ethan liked cars and cabs and the rush of the city. It was strange to think of him growing up in such a remote, small-town like the one he described.

She waited until her cousin had disappeared into the kitchen to start on the muffins and scones before carefully sliding the newspaper from her handbag. She supposed it was old fashioned to look for jobs through the classifieds anymore, but she was grasping for hope here, and she needed to keep all her options open. In the week since she'd been let go from the jewelry store, she'd found only five jobs to apply for, and with each day that ticked by without a phone call, her anxiety grew.

She swept her eyes over the ads, pen poised, her heart thumping with hope at the first listing and then sinking with dread by the last. Unless she wanted to take up "dancing" or enter into a pyramid scheme, there didn't seem to be much to choose from. She was either over-qualified or under-qualified, or just not right for any job at all.

She chewed on her nail and stared out the window as the morning trickle to the "L" stop began. All those people, off to paying jobs, while she sat here in the window, envying the purpose they had to their day.

Someone was off to her job today, she thought with a start. The job she'd given up. They were sitting at her desk, chatting with her coworkers, working on projects she'd initiated . . .

Well, she thought, brightening. She did have purpose today, at least. In three hours, Ethan was picking her up and they were headed up to Grey Harbor. An entire weekend of distraction and fun awaited her. Yes, she had something to do today, and even if it wasn't exactly productive, it sure as heck beat sitting in Hailey's apartment, imagining the words Matt might use to propose to the woman he'd always loved, or wondering how she would pretend to have been at work all day when Hailey arrived home.

That was the worst part. And she couldn't keep it up much longer.

"What do you think of those chairs?" Hailey asked as she came back into the storefront, tying an apron at her waist.

"These?" Claire frowned and looked down at the simple wooden chair. "I've never thought about them. Why?"

"I was just thinking of refreshing the place a bit. Maybe adding more color. Changing the light fixtures. Getting some new artwork." Hailey set her hands on her hips and looked around the space. Claire did the same, from the large glass display case to the gleaming espresso machine. The ceilings were tall, covered in decorative tin, and the far wall was made of exposed brick. The few tables were a rich medium brown wood, similar to the floorboards, but despite the dark furnishings, the light from the windows gave the space a warm and cozy feel.

"I like it. Don't change it. There's been too much change recently."

She hadn't ever come to the Corner Beanery back when she'd been with Matt, or even before she'd first met him. Her job in the South Loop was too far from Lincoln Park, and her apartment on the near west side made it equally inconvenient. Since moving into the neighborhood, she considered the small café to be her home away from home. A happy bustling place that Matt would never come to.

Probably, she thought, darting her eyes to the window. Technically, he could now be living in Lincoln Park, walking to the Armitage station at this very moment.

She felt shaky as she pushed her chair back and walked over to the counter. The chances were low, she told herself. No point in even worrying about it.

Still, it was nice to know she would be going out of town for the weekend.

Hailey stared thoughtfully at the far wall. "I was thinking of painting out the brick. White. Giving it an airy feeling."

Claire considered this. "It would be pretty. Think about it first before you rush into anything, though. Once you do it, you can't undo it."

"Careful Claire." Hailey laughed, teasing her with a

decade-old nickname Claire had been given for refusing to skip gym class in lieu of a trip to the mall junior year of high school. Even though Mr. Bateman never took attendance, one could never be too careful, Claire had told her friends, who rolled their eyes and had their fun without her.

More like reckless Claire, she thought now. Impulsive Claire. The old Claire never would have lost her job. But then, the old Claire never would have quit it either. Not without something lined up.

"It's not like I need to worry about it now, anyway. All my ideas for this place cost money, and I don't have any at the moment." Hailey shrugged. "Better go check on those muffins before the chaos hits. On second thought, mind getting the coffee started for me?"

Claire nodded silently. It was the least she could do for her cousin, considering she wasn't even paying rent. She felt sick to her stomach as she ground the rest of the beans and started three brews: robust, medium, and decaf. She was just beginning to think she should leave and busy herself with packing for the trip when there was a knock at the door.

Claire turned to see her friend Mary Harris smiling and waving through the glass door, her hair pulled back in a ponytail that was nearly as perky as her floral sundress. With one last press of a button, she hurried from behind the counter and crossed the room to turn the locks, excited to see a familiar face.

"You're here early today," Claire commented. "I just

put the coffee on."

"I wanted to see Lila before I went to the shop. It's going to be a hot one today and I'm expecting a record turnout this weekend." Mary beamed as she set her handbag on the counter, causing several slips of paper covered with what Claire knew to be ice-cream recipe ideas to spill onto the glass surface.

"Lila's not here yet," Claire said, but she would be soon, and she was looking forward to it. Hailey had offered up more than just a place to crash when Claire had so hastily thrown away her life. She'd also introduced her to women who had quickly become her friends, too.

"What do you think about Berry Jubilee for July's flavor of the month?" Mary suddenly asked, her eyes gleaming as they usually did when she started thinking of new flavors for her ice cream parlor, Sunshine Creamery. "I was thinking it would be a vanilla base with blueberries and cherries."

"Very red, white, and blue." Claire pulled a mug from the shelf as the coffee began to percolate, and then, on second thought, took two. She had hours to pack, and a little time with friends did wonders for her mood.

"What's red, white, and blue?" Lila asked as she closed the door behind her. She checked her watch and then turned the locks. Claire smiled her thanks across the room.

"A new ice cream flavor. Ben thought it would all turn purple, but I have my methods."

"Ben." Lila winked up at Claire and then smiled back at her younger sister. "And how is Ben these days?"

Mary gave a dreamy smile at the mention of her boyfriend. "Wonderful as ever. The house might even be ready by August. Violet can't wait to see her new room. It's going to be pink, of course, but I talked her into a touch of mint for variety."

"If things keep up like this, you'll be planning your wedding next. I'm sure little Violet would love to be a flower girl for her father's wedding." Lila sighed. "Three more weeks until Sam and I tie the knot. I can't believe how much can change in a year."

I can, thought Claire. A year ago she had life all figured out. Now . . .

"Coffee, Lila?" she asked abruptly, eager to change the subject and keep her thoughts on track.

"Please." Lila settled onto a counter stool beside Mary. "How's the new job?"

It took Claire a moment to realize that the question had been directed at her. Her hands stilled as she reached for another mug, and she took a moment to compose herself before replying, "Fine, fine." She kept her eyes trained on the coffee maker. She couldn't turn around and look them in the eye. It was hard enough to skirt Hailey's friendly inquisition, but to lie to her friends as well?

"Claire's going away for the weekend," Hailey announced as she pushed through the kitchen door carrying a plate of blueberry muffins topped with crumbly streusel. "With Ethan." Her lips twisted into a little smile.

Claire rolled her eyes. "It's not like that." She slid the steaming mugs to Lila and Mary. "He has a family wedding. I've agreed to go as his date."

Mary's eyebrows shot up. "His date?"

"More like his babysitter," Claire clarified. "There was some trouble with his family at his sister's wedding last summer."

Lila stirred a packet of creamer into her coffee. "Tell me a time when Ethan isn't causing trouble."

Claire laughed. It was all in good fun, she knew, and Ethan did have quite the reputation. And yes, he did cause his fair bit of trouble. But never with her.

At least that was one thing she could count on.

*

Two and a half hours later, Claire studied the contents of her suitcase with a critical eye. They'd be gone for four nights, returning on Sunday evening, and by her estimation she'd packed for a two-week vacation.

Still, she thought, Hailey would be thrilled to have a little more closet space for a few days, so really, it was the right thing to do.

Claire added another day dress to the pile and hesitated. It was just like Ethan to be so vague about the whole thing, only mentioning the possibility of a formal rehearsal dinner when prodded, and glossing over the wedding brunch as if it were nothing more than a trip to a diner. Claire added one last pair of sandals to the bag, wedging them in as best she could, and sighed.

Better overly prepared than under prepared, she thought, closing it shut and yanking the zipper. She'd always been a bit Type A, always the one who studied in advance, not crammed for an exam. Always the one who made lists, scratched things off, set goals and met them. She was a planner. Right up until all her plans blew up.

She pulled the zipper tight. Right, well, no use thinking about that now. Or the fact that the past week had produced no new leads in the career department. Or that she was running out of places to hide during the day when she was supposedly still at the jewelry store. Or that she felt sick to her stomach every time Hailey nicely asked how her day had gone. She was going away for the weekend, she would clear her head, have a few laughs, put some distance between herself and this city. And when she got back, she'd be ready to tackle her new life properly. And this time, well, this time she'd get it right. And that started with one promise: No more unsuitable men.

Claire scribbled a friendly good bye note to Hailey and tucked it under the fruit bowl on the counter, grabbing two bananas from the pile as she walked to the front door and slipped on her flip-flops, hoping she could manage the suitcase down the winding stairs without slipping. She hesitated only briefly, wondering if she should clear out a few items, and then decided there was no time, not unless she wanted to make the apartment a mess in her rush, and that wouldn't be fair to Hailey, who Claire suspected was looking nearly as forward to having this apartment to herself for a few days as Claire was happy to be getting away from it.

Ethan was already in the front of her building when she emerged, sweaty and a little exhausted, a few minutes later, the suitcase bumping along behind her.

"I would have carried that down for you," he remarked, stepping out of the car to pop the trunk, the hazard lights blinking.

"And where were you going to find parking at this hour?" she replied, motioning to the cab that was struggling to get through the narrow, one-way street. He gestured with impatience and honked on the horn twice to underscore his annoyance. Claire turned to Ethan. "We'd better be on with it."

"I suppose we should," Ethan said, frowning as he slammed the trunk closed.

Claire slid into the passenger seat and waited for him to turn off the street before asking, "Okay. What's going on?"

Ethan shifted gears as he approached the next intersection, his gaze never shifting from the road. "Nothing is going on."

She tipped her head, giving him a coy look, even though she knew he didn't see it. "Please. I can read you like a book. Now what is it? Another break-up?"

He snorted. "I'll have you know that I've been celibate

since Marla."

"An entire week!" Claire hooted. She didn't say how long it had been for her; it was obvious anyway. She hadn't dated since Matt had left her standing in a half-empty apartment with nothing to say and nowhere to go. But at least she had people to turn to, even if she hated having to lean on them.

"It's not that unusual," Ethan said, his jaw tightening as he pushed through a yellow light.

"Are we in a hurry?" Claire asked, resisting the urge to reach for the door handle.

"Hardly," Ethan said wryly. "In fact, I was hoping to drag out the inevitable for as long as possible."

"I thought you liked your family!" Claire said in surprise.

"Never said I didn't. But weddings aren't my thing."

"Oh, and here I would have thought you'd see them as tromping grounds. A room full of desperate women, hoping to catch the bouquet…"

He slanted her a glance. "More like a room full of women hoping to catch a groom. Uh-uh. No thank you."

Claire rolled her eyes and reached into her handbag for her sunglasses. "Well, I suppose it's a good thing I'm tagging along then. You're safe with a date."

"I am," Ethan said, looping his wrist over the steering wheel. "Thanks again for agreeing to it."

"Consider the favor all mine," Claire said, waving away his concern. "I feel better already, just knowing I get out of town for a while. I have a feeling Hailey is excited, too.

She doesn't let on, but I know my presence is, well, cumbersome."

"It's a small apartment," Ethan agreed. "How'd she react to you staying on a bit longer?"

Claire chewed on her nail and stared out the window, saying nothing.

"You haven't told her yet?" Ethan was incredulous. "What have you been doing all day when you are supposedly at work?"

"Looking for a job, of course!" She would become a waitress if she had to—the tips would be good, even if her time in the café had proven that she was hopeless at things like foaming milk or even carrying trays without her arms shaking and the dishes clattering.

"If you don't tell her soon, she's going to figure it out," Ethan warned.

"I know." Claire sighed. Hailey would be mad, but she would also be forgiving. She was kind like that. Just another reason Claire didn't want to disappoint her, not when she'd given her so much already. Without Hailey . . .Claire couldn't even think about it. "I'll get a job," she said firmly. "I had a job. I can get another one. I'm experienced. I'm determined."

"That's the Claire I've missed!" Ethan leaned over and patted her knee. It was quick, and casual, but not fast enough to stop the flurry of butterflies from ripping through her stomach. Claire stiffened and looked out the window, accidentally making eye contact with a middle-aged man in the next car. She looked down at her bare legs, shielded by her cotton skirt, and silently scolded herself. After this weekend she'd create a dating profile, get out there again. It was clearly time to move on. To find someone appropriate. And Ethan was not appropriate.

For God's sake, he was her best friend!

Her very cute, very unsuitable best friend, she thought, eyeing him. Yes, in a perfect world, he might have been the ideal man for her—if he wasn't shagging half of Chicago.

She fished through her bag again and found a banana. "Hungry?"

Ethan wrinkled his nose. "We'll stop along the way for something."

"Another stall tactic, I see." She slid him a smile.

Ethan hesitated, his eyes firmly on the road. "Look, I should warn you—"

"Oh, that's right. Your sister." All at once, Claire remembered Ethan's stories about his sister Amelia, who, at the age of thirty-four, was still struggling with the dating scene. Claire remembered a vague story about an unfortunate break-up timed just before their younger sister's wedding last summer. No doubt things were very tense right now. "Has she . . .found someone?"

"Nope. She's too busy holding out hope for some jerk who doesn't deserve her." He slid to a stop at the red light. "You two have a lot in common, now that I think about it."

Claire dropped the banana back into the bag. "I'll have you know I'm doing quite well lately. *Quite* well," she said again, with greater emphasis. After all, she'd barely thought about Matt once today, and that was only because of the darn banana. She hated them, but Matt loved them, and she was still buying them out of habit.

There was a long pause. "Good to know you're so much improved since the last time I saw you just seven days ago."

"Well, a lot can happen in a week," Claire replied, and she should know. In seven days you could go from planning your new life to having it ripped out from under you, to being single to meeting your soul mate.

My, that was optimistic of her. Yes, she must be feeling better. In no time at all, she'd make it through an entire day without wondering which part of the city Matt was living in, and what his new/old girlfriend looked like.

"So you're telling me that since you ran into him at the jewelry store, you haven't thought of Matt at all? Haven't wondered where he's living, haven't considered a drive-by at night, when the lights are on and the curtains are still open?"

Claire firmed her mouth. Busted.

"Ah-ha!" Ethan slammed a palm on the steering wheel, his laughter loud. "See, that's the problem, Claire. I know you too well. You can't lie to me, you know."

"I never try," Claire smiled, leaning back in her seat.

The engine revved as Ethan accelerated onto the

highway. "Don't worry, Claire. By the end of this weekend, Matt will just be a thing of the past. I promise."

*

It was half-past twelve by the time they found a place to stop for lunch: a ramshackle diner across the street from a gas station somewhere over the Wisconsin border. Claire climbed out of the car, stretching her long legs and smoothing her skirt with both hands, looking anything but impressed.

"I'm guessing you don't bring your dates to joints like this," she said, pursing her lips in that knowing way of hers.

"Hey, it's this or the truck stop," Ethan said, gesturing to their other option across the road.

"Well, it's certainly an adventure," Claire sighed, lifting her handbag onto her shoulder as she headed for the building.

Ethan locked the car and quickened his step to hold the door for her, releasing a blast of cold air as she passed inside.

Claire shivered and gestured to the back of the room, away from the window-box air-conditioner units. Ethan nodded his agreement, his stomach starting to knot with dread. They were just two hours from Door County now, and there was no telling how she would react to his announcement. He'd told himself that it was no big deal, he'd casually mention it in one of their usual daily phone conversations, but a week had passed since the initial invitation and now here they were, sliding into a booth with ripped vinyl, face to face with only a greasy Formica table to separate them, and his mother and sisters no doubt wringing their hands and circling the house, eager to meet Claire—his supposedly serious girlfriend.

Claire tucked a wisp of blond hair behind her ear and studied the menu. "I think I'll have a double cheeseburger," she announced as she closed it firmly.

Ethan grunted and looked up at her, incredulous. "You're kidding, right?"

"I eat salads, fruit, and yogurt every day of my life. This weekend is my little break from reality. Why shouldn't I indulge?"

Ethan shrugged. He couldn't argue with that.

"Two double-cheeseburgers," he told the waitress when she appeared at their table, pen poised. "And a chocolate shake."

"Two chocolate shakes," Claire said, winking at him.

Something in him tightened at the sight of her slow, secretive smile, but he pushed it firmly into place. Claire was special. She was his friend. At least for the moment.

He pulled in a breath. Time to tell her.

"So this wedding. I should warn you—"

Claire leaned forward, shaking her head. "You don't need to warn me, Eth. I know your sister's a little—"

"Crazy?" he finished.

Claire laughed good-naturedly. "I wasn't going to use that word, but okay, yes. I do now remember something about a tattoo of her ex's name."

On her upper arm. For all the world to see. Ethan muttered his disapproval under his breath. "Amelia is crazy. Boy crazy. Crazy. But you know all that."

Claire tipped her head. "Then what do you need to warn me about? Oh, God, you're not trying to set me up?" Her face turned pale as her eyes widened. "You know I hate set-ups, Ethan. Please, don't."

His laugh felt a little hollow. "It's not a set-up." *Well, not exactly*, he thought, running his hand through his hair in agitation.

Claire set a hand to her chest and leaned back in the booth. "Thank goodness for that. For a second there I thought you were bringing me up here on false pretenses." She grinned at him, but he didn't smile back. She blinked. "Ethan?"

He studied his tented hands on the table. He didn't know why he was making such a big deal of this. It was no big deal, really. At least he didn't think so. Claire, however . . .

"It's just . . .You know the stories I've told you. What happened last year at my sister Leslie's wedding . . ." He eyed her as their milkshakes were delivered to the table.

Claire peeled the paper back from her straw and took a long sip. "Something to do with the maid of honor, as I recall? Leslie's best friend?"

Ethan felt his jaw twitch, just like it did every time he thought of that night. How was he to know that the girl had crushed on him for fifteen years? He'd explained to his sister that he hadn't intended to lead her on, but from the fire in her eyes followed by the six months of silence, something told him she hadn't believed him.

Ah, Leslie. Just another obstacle he'd have to deal with this weekend.

"Look, my family thinks I should settle down. They think I . . . well, they worry about me." He frowned at his milkshake. "They think I'm . . ."

"A womanizer?" Claire asked pertly, one eyebrow cocked. "Sorry, I know you hate that word. Should I say...a Casanova?" She grinned and started to giggle.

Despite himself, Ethan managed a wry grin. "Yes, I suppose they think I'm a womanizer."

"And this bothers you because?" Claire plucked the cherry from the top of the whipped cream and brought it to her mouth, grasping it between her teeth before finally plucking the stem free.

Ethan stared at her in silence, unable to tear his gaze away. He could do with some ice water. Where was that waitress?

"I'm not a womanizer," he clarified, ignoring her doubtful expression. "I enjoy my single life, and I enjoy women's company."

Claire was just nodding her head, a funny smile playing at her lips.

"My family is worried . . ." Worried that he'd taint another family wedding. Worried that he'd be single forever. Worried about the reasons behind it. "I'm getting tired of listening to them fret."

"And?" Claire frowned. "I'm sorry, Ethan, I'm not following."

He pulled in a breath. Here it went. "I told them I was bringing you—"

"Of course," Claire interrupted. "I wouldn't want to spring myself on them!"

God, she wasn't making this easy. "I told them I was bringing you as my date." There, it was out.

Claire didn't blink for an unnatural amount of time. "You told them I was your *date?*" She spoke slowly, clarifying each word, her expression unreadable.

"Well, technically I told them you were my girlfriend," he said, sliding her one of those grins that usually got him out of trouble with women, but Claire's nostrils simply flared and her cheeks went a little pink as her eyes blazed bluer than ever.

Aw, crap. He should have known moves like that didn't work on Claire.

She leaned into the table, lowering her voice. "You told them I'm your girlfriend. So you lied to them, and you expect me to lie to them too."

Well, when she put it like that…

"We're doing them a favor, Claire," Ethan protested, feeling his conviction grow. It was true, he knew, thinking of how overjoyed his mother was when he mentioned his nonexistent relationship.

He closed his eyes for a second. *It's for the best*, he told himself. It was really the only way.

Claire clucked her tongue and pulled back from the table. "More like you're using me to cover your butt. What are you, five years old? Afraid of getting in trouble?" She slurped at her milkshake, her eyebrows pinched.

Ethan pushed his own drink away. "It wasn't like I concocted a scheme behind your back. I thought if you were there we could hang out, that it would be just like usual, and yes, that my mother would be forced to keep her unsolicited advice to herself if a guest was present. But then I told her I was bringing you and, well, she jumped to conclusions."

"Conclusions you didn't correct," Claire said sternly.

Ethan held up his palms. "She was so excited, and I hated to upset her. I figured . . . what harm is it? We'll go up, have a pleasant time, and when the time is right, I can say we broke up."

Claire held up a finger. "You can say that I broke up with you."

Ethan gave her a hard look. "You're kidding, right?" But her eyes flashed and those nostrils flared again, and so he said, "Okay. You broke up with me. We'll say it didn't work out. She won't be surprised," he muttered.

Claire sighed, and the table fell silent as the waitress slid their plates across the table. There was one ketchup bottle on the table and they reached for it at the same time. Ethan pulled away; a small gesture, but the least he could do.

"You have more fries than me," Claire sniffed, gesturing to his plate.

"You want to switch?"

Claire gave a small smile and Ethan felt his shoulders relax. He was used to women being mad at him, screaming, shouting, crying accusations. But something about Claire being upset with him felt different. Wrong, and scary.

He stiffened. He'd be best to remember that.

"I booked us two rooms at the hotel," he assured her. "I even asked for lake views. I'll see if I can upgrade you to a suite." He sounded desperate, but hell, he was desperate. Desperate to get his family off his back, desperate to go for a few days in his hometown without being reminded of the reasons that kept him away.

Claire salted her fries. "I suppose it's not that big of a deal," she said, "other than the fact that we're lying to your entire family."

"We're protecting them," he insisted.

"You're protecting yourself," she snorted. She cut her burger down the middle, even though he'd already gripped his in two hands. "I suppose it's too late to turn back now, though. You have impeccable timing, Ethan." She lifted an eyebrow, her lips pursed, but there was a sheen of amusement in her gaze that told him he had her.

"I owe you, Claire," he grinned, sinking his teeth into his burger as his appetite returned.

Claire locked his gaze. "Yes. You do. Big time. But you have to promise me one thing before I agree to this."

Ethan struggled to swallow his food. He should have known. Claire was stubborn and hard-headed. Traits he usually loved about her. "What's that?"

"No funny business."

His pulse kicked as he laughed and picked up a few fries, but her warning was a good one, and one that he should heed. Claire was the closest thing to a real relationship he'd had in . . . well, years. He'd felt the sting of loss before, and he'd be damned if he felt it again.

And Claire, however perfect and pretty and funny and sweet she may be, was the last person in the world he could ever get involved with.

"No funny business," he said firmly. Definitely, no funny business. Ever.

Chapter Four

As soon as they turned into the lakeside town of Grey Harbor, Claire knew that Ethan hadn't done his hometown justice. The streets were lined with quaint shops and iron benches, and flowers seemed to burst from planters on every corner. As the street turned residential, Claire smiled at quaint homes tucked behind white picket fences.

The Parker home wasn't too far from town, set serenely at the base of a gravel paved driveway that seemed to lead straight to the waterfront. Overgrown hydrangeas hedged by a stone path led up to the large, cedar-sided Victorian home, where a boxwood wreath hung proudly on the freshly painted blue front door.

Claire and Ethan didn't speak as they climbed the porch steps, but she was all too aware of the tightness in his jaw, the nervous thing he was doing with his hands, and the telltale change in his breathing. The man was nervous as hell, but something told her it wasn't about this ruse. No, it was something else. Something she couldn't put her finger on.

Despite her circumstances, she was oddly curious. Really, could his family be that bad?

"Are you going to knock?" She realized that they had been hovering on the wraparound porch for an unnatural amount of time, given that this was Ethan's home and all.

"No, I'll just . . ." He reached for the brass door handle at the same time the door was flung open, and there, gathered in the narrow frame, were at least six women of various heights, ages, and hair colors, ogling at Claire with naked glee.

"She's real," Claire heard someone hiss, and suddenly she was being enveloped in someone's arms as a peal of joy went out, and all at once, everyone was talking over everyone else, making it impossible to decipher any clear words, but the tone was one of unmistakable excitement.

Claire finally untangled herself from the woman's arms, only to have her hands gripped tightly. "I'm Barbara, Ethan's mother." Her wide hazel eyes roved Claire's face with overt interest as a pleased smile teased her mouth. "But then you can probably see that. Everyone says he takes after me!"

It was true. She had the same dark hair, same eyes and square jawline. Claire suddenly wondered what Ethan's father looked like, but she knew better than to ask. It was a sore subject, and one he didn't dwell on, and Claire understood, now more than ever. It wasn't easy to lose a parent, regardless of your age.

"And this is Leslie, our youngest," Barbara pushed a dark-haired girl to the front of the group. Even though they were the same age, Claire couldn't stop herself from staring at the small baby bump, suddenly feeling like she was a child, with a long road to go before she found herself in such a position, especially now.

Unlike Ethan, Leslie's eyes were dark and unreadable, but her smile was rueful when she lifted her gaze to her brother. "Planning on behaving yourself this weekend, Ethan?"

Ethan gave a good-natured laugh, but his cheeks looked a little ruddy, Claire thought. "I always do."

Leslie snorted and extended her hand.

"I'll keep him in line," Claire assured her, and Leslie's eyes lit with surprise.

"I like this one," she said, flashing her first grin, and Claire decided on the spot that she liked Leslie too. In fact, she liked them all, even though there were so many of them, and they were still staring, and it was a little nerve-racking, really.

"Where's Amelia?" Ethan suddenly asked.

Barbara's expressed turned worried. "She's not feeling well. I told her not to worry. She'll meet up with everyone later."

Ethan passed Claire a knowing look, subtle enough to

go undetected by the rest of the group, who were now ushering them through a large entranceway to the back of the house, where huge kitchen windows lent a breathtaking view of a stone patio, green grass, and blue water.

"Lemonade?" Barbara asked, already pouring two glasses and handing them out.

Claire happily accepted her own and took a sip. "This is a lovely house you have," she admired, walking to the bay window to take in a better view. A wicker conversation set was wedged under the shade of a weeping willow, where a woman sat with her feet curled up, reading a book, and, from what Claire could tell, smoking a cigarette.

Amelia, she thought, suddenly intrigued.

"Oh, well, it's been in the family forever. When I was little it was our summer home, but when my parents passed away, we decided to make Grey Harbor our full-time residence. Not that Ethan has noticed," she added, giving him a pointed look.

"Life gets busy, Mom. Besides, I wasn't exactly welcome with open arms during my last visit." He frowned into his glass as the room fell silent.

Barbara wrung her hands nervously, and flicked her eyes from Leslie to Claire. "Now, where are my manners? Let me introduce you to everyone. You've met Leslie, of course, and this is Milly, my oldest sister, and Patricia, my younger sister. Her daughter Meryl is the one getting

married. And this is my cousin Ellen, and her daughter
Lydia, and my aunt Hazel," she said, wrapping an arm
around a frail woman wearing a thick wool cardigan,
despite the warm day.

Claire shook each woman's hand and stood back,
letting the awkward silence resume.

"I must say it was quite a surprise when Ethan said he
was bringing a guest. Our Ethan is just full of secrets, it
seems." His mother winked at him.

You could say that again, Claire thought.

"Ethan said you've been dating since Christmas!"
Barbara exclaimed, and a murmur of approval went up in
the group.

Claire shot Ethan a murderous glance. "Did he now?"

"Said you worked at an auction house!"

"I have some antiques in my attic you might be
interested in seeing," interrupted Hazel. "My daughter
calls them junk, so I'd be quite interested to see what an
expert has to say."

"Mother." Ellen sighed.

"There are so many antique shops in town!" Barbara
said excitedly. "Ethan will take you, won't you, Ethan?"

Ethan's eyes were flicking from female relative to
female relative, and for a moment, Claire felt a pang of
sympathy for him, but only for a moment. After all, the
man was lying to these poor women, creating a fictitious
life they were clearly tickled over.

"Well, we should probably get settled at the hotel,"
Ethan began, but his mother barely gave him a glance.

"Pshaw. No son of mine is going to stay in a hotel, not when we have so much room! Now, Leslie and Nick are staying in the house, and Amelia, of course," Barbara added somewhat darkly. "I figured you two would like a little space, so I went ahead and made up the guest cottage for you. There are fresh linens on the bed and towels in the cupboard next to the tub." She beamed at Claire, whose pulse skipped with panic.

The bed? As in, only one?

"Oh, but we can't impose," she tried, hearing the strain in her voice.

Barbara took the empty glass from Claire's hand and splashed more lemonade into it. "Nonsense! It's not every day my son brings a girlfriend home, and I must admit, we're all quite eager to get to know you a little better." She winked at Ethan, who seemed to be radiating tension Claire had never witnessed in him before.

"Now don't go scaring her away," Ethan warned.

Claire dragged her eyes to his, holding them there. Now that was rich.

"But it's a beautiful cottage!" cried Milly, who was identifiable by her many strands of pearls and matching earrings. She was older than Barbara by several years, it seemed, and had a wild look in her eyes. "Barbara rents it out for a pretty penny nearly every week of the year. Lots of honeymooners enjoy the amenities." She winked, and Claire felt her teeth graze into some semblance of a smile.

Ethan stepped forward. "Really, Mom. We're fine at

the hotel. We don't want to take away the room from a paying guest."

Claire mentally fist-pumped. An excellent point—surely his mother couldn't argue with that.

But Barbara just handed Claire the glass of lemonade with a smile and said, "Now don't you worry. I cancelled this weekend's reservation the moment I heard about the wonderful Claire. Besides, you can't have your hotel room back. To compensate for the inconvenience, I gave the couple one of the rooms you'd booked at the hotel—I have connections like that. Two rooms, the front desk said." She clucked her tongue. "They must have made a mistake."

"Mom—" Ethan's voice had taken on a tone of warning, but Barbara was not to be deterred.

"I'm a modern woman, Ethan. I know how the world works now. In my day people waited for marriage, but then, in my day, people weren't still unattached in their thirties, either."

The older women of the group all exchanged knowing looks.

"Mom, I think Claire might be comfortable—"

"Oh, settle down, Ethan, I know when to back off, you know. And Claire knows what I'm referring to. Times have changed! And I pride myself on rolling with it! Besides, something tells me Claire and I are going to get along just fine," she said, looping her arms through Claire's as she led them out the back door and toward their honeymoon suite.

*

Amelia was still sitting on the old wicker bench when they approached the cottage, her tattoo on full display near the straps of her tank top. She set her book aside when Ethan said hello, her gaze immediately shifting to Claire with impassive interest. Ethan steeled himself as panic set in, wondering if this was such a good idea after all, if it might have been easier to face them all alone, put up with the insinuations and the warnings and even the threats, and then go on his way, back to the city, back to his life. Back to his ways, as they called it.

"So this is the woman we've heard all about," Amelia remarked, standing to smooth her long cotton skirt and extend a hand to Claire. "She seems normal," she accused, lifting an eyebrow at him.

Ethan balled a hand into a fist, but he could see Claire swallowing her laughter from his periphery. "And how are you, Amelia? Will I be meeting your wedding date this evening?"

As soon as the words came out, he regretted them. Amelia's eyes narrowed on him, and all at once she was grabbing her book, and making a big, clumsy show of leaving.

"Nice," Claire whispered, shaking her head at him in disapproval.

"Amelia!" Ethan called out at his older sister, who was scrambling barefoot up the stone steps to the back patio, her shoulders squared in fury. "Amelia, come on. I didn't mean to upset you!" But it was no use. She was sliding open the sunroom door without a glance back.

Well, great. He hadn't been home even fifteen minutes and already he was in trouble with at least one member of the family, when all he'd wanted for the weekend was to avoid it.

"She's on edge," his mother said. "We're all doing our best to tiptoe around her. I strongly suggest you do the same, Ethan. Between you and me, I think it's hard on her that you have . . . Claire."

Claire turned around and gave Ethan a hooded look.

Great. So now he was in trouble with at least two women on this stretch of property.

Ethan shoved his hands into his pockets and stared out at the lake. He couldn't help it; this place always put him in a bad mood. It made him out of sorts, irritable and agitated. He was on edge, saying things he shouldn't say.

He looked down at his shoes. Four more days. He could do it.

They hovered outside the cottage door while his mother showed off her new window boxes, and Ethan ground on his teeth, his gaze lingering on the sunroom doors of the main house, where no doubt Amelia was already regaling the rest of the group with his insensitive behavior.

But what about their insensitive behavior, he thought, feeling anger heat his blood. What about their little comments, their silent judgment, their sharp remarks?

God knew it was hard enough coming back here without their commentary.

He pulled in a breath and studied the back of Claire's head as she obediently leaned in to smell one of the daylilies. Her blond hair glistened in the sun, and his mother slid him a smile so approving, for a brief moment Ethan felt a twinge of guilt for lying to her.

But then he remembered the reason behind it. Thought of the reaction he'd received. The opinions they held.

The one he was hell-bent on changing this weekend.

"Well now, you probably want to freshen up and change before dinner," Barbara was saying as she unlocked the door and let them pass. Ethan saw the panic in Claire's eyes before he even felt it himself.

The room was smaller than he'd remembered. It was hardly a cottage at all, but more of a bedroom with an en suite bathroom and a kitchenette in one corner. French doors led to a small patio that housed two Adirondack chairs and a side table, but otherwise, the accommodations lent no other seating area. The bed was covered in a simple white duvet, queen-sized, as luck would have it, and Claire's eyes never strayed from it.

"I see you painted the walls," Ethan remarked, desperate to break the silence. Last time he was in here, they'd been a light green. But then, that was a long time ago, he supposed. Last summer he'd stayed in the main house. He couldn't recall his visit before then, he realized with a start.

His mother swept a hand over the dresser. "Grey blue. Reminds me of the fog rolling in on a summer evening. I added new throw pillows, as you can see."

Eventually, Claire blinked and murmured, "Beautiful. It's just beautiful. Is this the, uh, only cottage you have on the premises?"

"Oh, yes. It was an old boathouse before we converted it. See the rafters? Ethan used to climb those when he was little." Barbara chuckled and shook her head fondly at Ethan. "This boy always had a way of making trouble, but then, I suppose you know that already, Claire." She raised an eyebrow, and Claire shot him a look of naked amusement.

"So yes, just this one small cottage, but renters love it, and I hope you will, too. It's quiet down here, secluded, and don't you worry, I won't be knocking on the door to bug you two."

Ethan shifted uneasily on his feet, summing up the space on the floor. Thanks to a wide chest of drawers and two generous end tables, there was very little space in the room, certainly not enough to camp out on for a few nights.

He glanced at Claire again, imagining she was making the same calculation.

"Well, I'll leave you to it," his mother finally said. "Dinner is at six at Patricia's. Casual, on the beach, if the weather holds up." She crossed her fingers. "I know everyone is looking very forward to it," she added with emphasis, casting Ethan a meaningful glance.

"I'll just go get the luggage," Ethan said quickly, hoping to follow on his mother's tread, but Claire just smiled and said sweetly, "No, stay for a minute. The luggage can wait." Her gaze held his with such fury, that he knew he had no choice but to oblige.

He waited until his mother had closed the door behind her and was a safe distance back to the main house before turning back to her. "Look, I can explain."

Claire folded her arms across her chest and tipped her head. "Explain what exactly? The fact that we've supposedly been dating since Christmas? Or that I'm expected to carry on lying to all these nice women? Or maybe you'd just like to explain where exactly you'll be sleeping tonight, because we sure as hell aren't sharing this bed."

He frowned. "Why not? It's not like I'm going to cop a feel." He grinned, hoping to lighten the mood, but she was having none of it.

She sighed and dropped onto the bed. "Look, why don't we just tell them the truth? That you and I are good friends, that you brought me along as your date, that I'll keep you in line and make sure you don't disappear with the bride or anything between now and Saturday night."

"The bride is my cousin," he reminded her calmly.

"Fine, then the maid of honor." She tossed up her hands. "I thought we'd stay at a hotel. In separate rooms. That we'd casually see your family for a few minutes at the rehearsal dinner and the reception. Then we'd disappear into the crowd. But this?" She shook her head. "I can't do this, Ethan. I can't lie to these people. And I don't see how you can either."

"It's a white lie," he reminded her. "Besides, you have no trouble lying to your family."

Her cheeks turned red. "That's only temporary!"

"So is this!"

Claire clamped her mouth together, her breath was hard. "I plan to tell Hailey about losing my job when I need to. Until then . . . why worry her?"

"And I don't want to worry my family," Ethan said. "You saw the way they talked to me. Even the way they were with you. Imagine what I'd be hearing if you weren't with me? If they didn't think I'd changed my ways?" He gave her a long look, watching her waver. "I'm not doing this to hurt anyone. And if it makes you feel better, I'll sleep in the bathtub."

She laughed at this, and a glimpse of the old Claire, the girl he knew, the girl he loved, reappeared before his eyes.

He swallowed hard. Took one step backward toward the door. Right. Time to get the luggage.

He gulped in a big breath of the clean country air and hurried his way to the car, feeling the eyes of his extended female relationships on him through the back kitchen window. He didn't stop until he got to the car, sheltered by the side of the house where the windows were shielded by overgrown shrubs, and closed his eyes, pushing out the sights and the sounds and the memories that seemed to hit him everywhere he turned. He avoided this place for a reason, but not for the one Claire knew. His mother and sisters and nosy aunts, he could handle. But the feelings he had when he was here, the reminders of happiness, of loss . . . That he couldn't handle.

And that was why he needed Claire to stick with the plan. To keep him in line. To keep him from doing something far more stupid than having a fling with a member of the wedding party.

He opened his eyes, popped the trunk, and pulled out the luggage, cursing under his breath when he felt the weight of Claire's suitcase. Four days, and she may as well be taking a two-week trip abroad. Women, he thought, locking the doors, even though there was no around for a mile and he doubted they'd try to steal his radio.

Even though he'd grown up without a father, even though some claimed he was somewhat of an expert when it came to the other gender, the truth of the matter was that he didn't know the first thing about them.

And maybe that's why he was still single. Asking his best friend to pose as his girlfriend.

Because he couldn't find one on his own. And when he did—when he had . . . Well, no use thinking about that.

Claire was collecting towels from the linen chest when Ethan reentered the cottage.

"You don't have to sleep in the bathtub," she said, giving him a faint smile. "But there will be a roll of towels separating our bodies." She held up a pointer finger, locking his eyes. "I swear to God, one move, one finger crosses those towels, and the wrath of your sisters will pale in comparison to what you'll see from me."

He nodded and set the bags down in the corner.

"Four days, Eth. I mean it. And next time you talk to your mom, you tell her we've broken up, got it?"

He nodded. He got it. It was the kind of conversation he had a lot of experience with, unfortunately.

Chapter Five

Claire took her clothes and toiletries into the en suite bathroom and firmly locked the door behind her. Her heart was pounding, and she wasn't sure why. Normally she felt comfortable with Ethan, more comfortable than she did with Hailey half the time. She could say anything, do anything, didn't have to monitor herself around him, didn't have to watch her words or worry if she had food in her teeth or laughed too loud at a joke that wasn't all that funny.

But something about being here, out of the city, trapped in this tiny boathouse, made her start to feel prickly and weird, as if something was shifting between them, a heightened awareness she didn't exactly like.

She checked the knob, just to be sure it was indeed locked, and then stripped out of her clothes before turning the taps to the shower. It was a pretty bathroom, light and airy, with a skylight above the tub. She laughed as she closed the glass door to the shower, imagining Ethan curled up in there, with his pillow and blanket. With his six-foot athletic frame, it would no doubt be a tight squeeze. She supposed it was sweet of him to offer, but then that was Ethan. Thoughtful. Dependable. Readable. There was no mystery with Ethan. No pretense, no façade. She knew him inside out.

So why did she suddenly feel a flutter of nerves at the thought of him being on the other side of that door?

She hurried to shampoo her hair and rinse the day off her skin. Ever so hospitable, Barbara had left a stack of towels within arm's reach. Claire took the top one from the pile and wrapped herself with it, jumping when she heard the knock at the door.

"You decent?"

"What?" Her cheeks flared. "No! I'm not!" Panic caused her voice to screech, and even though she knew she had locked the door, she eyed the handle in horror, waiting for it to turn, for Ethan to walk in and see her . . . well, not decent.

"Well, hurry up! If we're late I'll never hear the end of it!"

Claire rolled her eyes as she towel-dried her hair. It was a warm evening, and there would be plenty of time for it to dry on its own before they went to the clam bake at Ethan's aunt's house. According to him, it was just a short walk down the beach. Claire set a hand to her stomach as fresh nerves pumped. More friends and families to fool. More lies to tell.

She slipped on the pale blue sundress she'd brought for the occasion and added a touch of makeup. She rarely wore much, especially in the summertime. Ethan said it was a casual affair, and, hoping that was the case, she wedged her toes into a pair of espadrilles and unlocked the bedroom door.

Ethan was lying on the bed—in the middle of the bed—when she opened it, the steam from the shower filling the small room.

"I see you forgot my rule about staying on your side," she observed, raising an eyebrow.

He had the nerve to look confused. "It's not bedtime yet. Besides, I needed to rest if I'm going to make it through this shindig tonight."

"Gee, I'm really looking forward to it now," Claire said, laughing slightly under her breath as she walked to her side of the bed and folded her dirty clothes into a bag in her suitcase.

"Oh, you'll have a great time," Ethan said with confidence.

"And why won't you?" she asked, looking up at him.

His mouth quirked into a lazy grin. "Easy. They're my family, not yours."

Ethan took more than half an hour to primp in the bathroom—nearly twice as long as it had taken Claire, who had shaved her legs and washed and conditioned her shoulder-length hair. And applied makeup.

When he finally emerged, he looked barely any different than when he'd entered. Claire pursed her lips to smother a smile. She loved Ethan, God did she, but the truth was there was a reason why Ethan could never settle down and fall in love—he was entirely too self-focused.

"If I'd known it would take you half the day, I would have skipped my shower," she quipped.

"Hey, you thought this afternoon was bad? You haven't seen the rest of the Parker clan. They can't wait to get their hands on me, to look for any reason to criticize. Do I have any nicks on my face? I shaved in a hurry."

She stood and peered at his chin. It was a very nice, strong, square chin. His body was still warm from the shower. His skin smelled like aftershave. She frowned. What was wrong with her?

"No nicks. Smooth as a baby." Well, not really. More like perfectly manly and sort of sexy and . . . wrong. She really needed to get out there again. Clearly, she was ready.

He looked down at his white linen shirt, frowning. "Should I tuck this in?"

"If you're tucking in that shirt, then I'm changing my dress," Claire said, adjusting the back of her earring.

"Sorry. I just . . . I get nervous around these people." He ran a hand through his hair, dragging in a shaky breath.

Claire laughed and reached over to take his arm. "These people are your family. How bad can it be?"

*

Fifteen minutes later, she knew exactly how bad the night might be. As they approached the spot of beach where a bonfire was already crackling and glowing, the music seemed to stop, and slowly, face after face stopped their conversation to stop and stare.

It seemed that the novelty of her arrival hadn't dimmed since this afternoon. If anything, it had spread to dozens of more people, who were now practically pushing each other aside to have a good look.

Claire felt her stride falter, and she didn't dare look at Ethan, who had stopped talking and was no doubt following her gaze.

"Here goes nothing," he muttered, and all at once, Claire felt his warm, smooth palm slide against hers.

"What are you doing?" she asked in panic, snatching her hand back. She stopped walking, aware that as she did so, every person on the beach was piquing with interest, craning their necks to see the lovers' quarrel that was unfortunately out of earshot.

He gave her a mild smile. "Claire, if we're going to make them believe we're a couple, we have to act like we're a couple."

She chewed her bottom lip. He had a point there. "Yes, but holding hands. It's so, so . . ." She hadn't held hands with anyone since Matt.

"Would you rather I put my hand around your waist?"

His lips twitched, and Claire realized he was having fun with this.

"I'm glad to see this is so easy for you!" She folded her arms across her chest defensively, but he just gave her a rueful smile in return.

"Lighten up, Claire. You know what your problem is? You take life too seriously."

"I do not!" she scoffed, but she did. She knew it. And leave it to Ethan to keep saying it.

"I mean, if you're worried I'm going to take advantage—"

"Ethan!" But now it was her turn to laugh. She did, but then remembering this ruse, turned from him, frowning. She hadn't thought ahead this far. She hadn't assumed there would be touching, or . . . She groaned.

"Look, it's a beautiful night. We're on the beach. We'll have a couple drinks, make a little small talk, and then we can go back to the cottage and put a big wall of towels between our two bodies."

"Ethan . . ." She sighed.

"Is it so hard to pretend to be attracted to me?" he asked, and for a moment Claire thought she saw a look of hurt soften his eyes. "If it makes it any easier, pretend that Matt is there. Give him something to turn green over."

Claire gave a little smile. Wouldn't that be the day?

"Fine," she said, gritting her teeth as she reached out her hand and let him take it. His grip was firm, his skin warm, and as they walked toward their waiting audience,

Claire had the strange feeling that she could sort of get used to this . . .

*

"So, together since the holidays!" Aunt Milly's eyes seemed to pop on the statement, as if she couldn't quite believe such a thing was even possible. "A solid six months!"

Claire looked up at him through a gritted smile and said sweetly, "That's right. Since New Year's Eve, actually."

They both knew how each of them had really spent New Year's—she'd gone to Vail with Matt and he'd gone to a masquerade party with that brunette with the long legs and the law degree. He was working on New Year's, covering the best events of the year, not that he minded. Half the time his job felt like play, at least the research aspect. And when he mentioned reservations at the hottest restaurant in town, it was usually the icebreaker he needed to secure a date for Saturday night.

Free drinks and the best tables weren't the only perks of his job. Still, if he was honest with himself, going out four nights a week was getting old.

"My, this certainly is promising," Milly continued, giving her husband Les, who seemed to be struggling to keep his eyes from drooping, a firm jab in the ribs. "I don't think Ethan has held onto a relationship for that long since—"

"Les, you doing okay?" Ethan cut in. He swallowed hard, and did his best at playfully giving his uncle a friendly slap on the back. "Another round of drinks is in order, I think. Claire, want to help?"

She smiled demurely, and hurried to follow him. Before they were out of earshot, Ethan heard Milly remark, "How sweet. They don't want to be apart, even for a few minutes."

Behind him, Claire snorted, and by the time they pushed their way to the drinks table, they were both laughing uncontrollably.

"What do you say we get out of here?" Ethan suggested.

"But, Les's drink?" Claire's eyes crinkled in confusion, but Ethan shrugged away her concern.

"Did you see him? The man was practically snoring on his feet. Once he settles onto a chair, he'll be out for the night. Poor guy is used to having his ear talked off." He shook his head.

He'd gotten used to it over the years, the buzz of chatter, the seemingly endless amount of time his mother and her sisters could sit and talk. He liked it, especially as a kid, on the cool summer nights when his mother cranked his bedroom windows open. He'd turn on his side and listen to their laughter, the din of their voices from the back patio, where they sipped iced tea and reminisced about the past. It made the night feel less dark, somehow, less lonely. It made him forget that his father wasn't there anymore.

Ethan turned to Claire, who was standing patiently at his side, staring out onto the water that lapped softly at the sand not far from her bare feet. Her sandals were dangling from her fingers, the hem of her dress billowing in the breeze, and for a moment, Ethan felt a sense of peace wash over him, the same way it had all those years ago when the breeze filtered through his bedroom windows and the murmur of voices began to emerge in the dusk.

Claire wasn't a chatterbox. If anything, she was quiet. He liked that about her.

He looked over his shoulder to where his mother was deeply engrossed in a conversation with his cousin Meryl and her fiancé, Eddie. He knew an opportunity when he saw one.

He grabbed Claire's hand again, sort of liking the excuse to hold it a little more than he should. It was small, light and feminine, but there was strength in it, and a security he hadn't felt in a while.

He pushed that thought away. No use going there, not when no good could come of it.

"Come on. We'll see enough of everyone over the next few days." He winked, and Claire's blue eyes sparkled as they turned and marched casually across the sand, through the mingling guests, and farther into the growing darkness, until the party was just a strange glow in the night, far behind them.

He dropped her hand, feeling a strange distance from

her when he did, and stared straight ahead, aware of her body next to his with every step. The big house that he'd grown up in loomed at the top of the dunes, just ahead. Ethan tipped his head toward it. "It's still early. Let's grab a drink."

They hurried the rest of the way to house, and Ethan didn't exhale until they were finally inside, the door closed firmly behind them. The house seemed quiet and eerily still without the usual boisterous activity that filled it. The light in the kitchen was still on, and Ethan grabbed a beer from the fridge, holding it out to Claire. She wrinkled her nose, as he knew she would, and he offered her the next best thing.

"A wine cooler?" She turned it over in her hand, mesmerized.

"It was that or hard lemonade. It appears all the wine has been rounded up for the festivities." He pulled open a drawer and found the bottle opener.

"I haven't had one of these since high school," Claire laughed, popping the top.

Intrigued, he leaned against the counter, studying her with interest. "You mean to tell me that you, Claire Wells, actually *drank* in high school?"

"I didn't *drink*." She flushed. "I mean, once. I went to a party one night with Hailey and . . . my friend's older sister was handing out wine coolers."

He grinned. "And let me guess, you got tipsy."

Claire pursed her lips. "I'm not such a good-goody, you know. We can't all be rebels like you."

"And is that what you think I am? A rebel?" He tipped the beer back, feeling the foam chase its way down his throat.

She shrugged. "Compared to me. Come on," she said, tugging his sleeve. "I want to see your room."

He hesitated, took another pull on his beer. "There's nothing to see in there but some old yearbooks."

As soon as he saw the delight in her face, he knew he'd said the exact wrong thing.

"Well, then I sure as heck can't miss this!" She was already off, down the hallway, before he could stop her, and, setting the beer down on the counter, he hurried after her, only to see her hurrying her pace, laughing as she bolted up the stairs. He tried to grab her arm, but she was too quick, and he grabbed a piece of her dress instead. She tripped, clambering up the stairs, laughing so hard he was laughing too. They were behaving like children, something he only did with Claire.

She stood at the top of the landing triumphantly, panting for breath. "Which way is it?" she asked.

He sighed, and vaguely motioned to the left. There was no use resisting the inevitable. When Claire set her mind to something, she usually found a way to see it through. "Last door. You can't miss it."

The baseball pinup was still on the wood paneled door, and Claire tapped it with a finger, jutting her bottom lip at him to show how adorable she thought it was, and pushed open the door.

He shoved his hands into his pockets and hovered in the door jamb. He hadn't been in this room since he was a kid—now when he came back, he usually stayed in one of the guest rooms with the bigger beds. This room was a capsule, of a different time, a different place. A different person.

"I don't know why, but I assumed there would be some bikini pinups or something," Claire joked, admiring the baseball posters that framed the two big windows with a view of the lake. She walked over to his desk, leaning down to study the framed pictures his mother had kept all these years.

"Oh." She gave a sad smile as she picked one up to study, and Ethan felt his blood still for a moment. He knew the photo, knew it well. It was one of the last memories he had of his father, a day on the lake, like so many others. He was eight in the photo, and he had a cast on his arm from falling out of a tree. He'd taken that day for granted, assumed that life would always be carefree, that people didn't just leave you, but they did. Whether they were taken from you or they left on their own accord, nothing in life lasted forever.

He eyed Claire, thinking of the tears she'd shed when her mother had died. He'd sat by her side, not knowing what to do or what to say, but somehow he knew that was enough for her. He understood. Not everyone did. That alone was some comfort, he supposed.

"You resemble him," she said, her smile a little hesitant, but something about the comment, the new perspective, made Ethan feel like just for a fleeting moment, a part of his father was alive again. "It's the mouth. And the nose."

He swallowed hard, wanting her to put the photo down almost as much as he wanted her to keep talking. He never spoke of his father—at first it seemed too cruel, too insensitive toward his mother—but now, it was he who kept quiet when the man's name was brought up, he who felt the strain of loss every time he walked into this house.

Finally, Claire set the photo back on the desk, exactly where she'd found it. She was thoughtful that way, always careful not to overstep.

"Now where are those yearbooks you promised to show me?" She tapped a finger against her mouth, looking around the room.

"Hey, I never promised you that," he said, flinching on the words for a moment. He never promised anything, but somehow, with Claire, it was always different. He gave in, didn't resist, but then, she was different than other women. Different than most people.

He made a grand show of sighing. "They're in the bottom drawer of the bedside table. Don't laugh," he warned.

Claire eagerly crouched down to retrieve the stack of books, starting with his freshman year and working in chronological order. She hooted in laughter when she saw his braces and bowl cut. "You were on the *debate* team?"

she asked, eyes popping, as she stared up at him. "I don't know why I envisioned you as football quarterback instead."

"I might have inflated my role on the football team," Ethan said ruefully.

"It charms the ladies, right?" Claire shook her head, smiling as she flipped to the next page. Ethan dropped beside her on the bed, taking in her familiar sweet scent that mingled with the warm summer air. The old house still didn't have air-conditioning, and crickets croaked from the half-open window, filling the room with all those summer smells and sounds you didn't find back in the city.

He relaxed as she flicked through the book, getting caught up in the memories himself.

"Do you ever keep in touch with anyone?" Claire asked, moving on to his senior yearbook.

Ethan tensed. "Oh, a few that still live in town. The rest have moved on. You know how it is."

"Who's the girl?" she asked, leaning forward to study the picture with interest.

"Oh, just a prom date," Ethan said coolly, but inside his blood was on fire. His chest began to pound as he waited for her to turn the page. He didn't want to look at that picture, didn't want to remember that face.

"She's pretty," Claire remarked. "Another heart you broke along the way?"

Ethan smiled tightly. "Something like that," he managed.

Only it was nothing like that. And it wasn't something he wanted to discuss. Even with Claire.

"I left my drink downstairs," he said, suddenly needing to be out of that room, away from the small single bed and the photos and . . . all of it.

She looked up at him in surprise. "Okay."

"Can I get you anything?" He was already walking to the door, eager to be away.

"No," she said, closing the yearbook. "But I think I'll come down with you. I've embarrassed you enough for one night."

"Just wait until the bachelorette party," Ethan laughed in an attempt to lighten his mood. "I don't even want to know the things my sisters will be sharing with you then."

He suddenly stopped walking, his chest tightening when he considered his statement. But no, he told himself firmly as he slowly walked down the stairs. No, surely even his sisters knew better than to bring up that . . .

At least, he could only hope.

Chapter Six

Claire opened one eye, and then, ever so slowly, the other, only releasing her pent-up breath when she noticed the towel was safely wedged between her body and Ethan's, and that he was wearing a T-shirt, and hopefully some kind of pants, although given his exasperating and endless desire to rattle her up, she didn't dare test the waters by tugging on the blanket.

She rolled out of bed and smoothed her hair. Despite the unseasonably warm weather and the lack of so much as a lakeside breeze all night long, she'd worn the most modest pajamas she owned—flannel pants and a matching long-sleeved collared shirt, buttoned all the way to the very top, thank you very much—and now the thick material stuck to her skin.

The windows were open, not that they'd helped, but

now Claire opened the French doors and stepped onto the patio, hoping some morning country air would cool her head.

Last night had been strange, and it wasn't just because she'd held another man's hand for the first time since Matt. She was struggling with how . . . *natural* it felt to stand side by side with Ethan at the party, to laugh with his family members, to exchange secret smiles with him as they sipped their drinks. She picked up a rock from the edge of the patio and skipped it into the water.

Ridiculous. Of course it felt natural with Ethan. He was her closest friend. She knew him. She was comfortable around him.

So why did her stomach start to knot every time she thought of the way it felt to stand beside him, and have him look at her like that—like she was more than just a friend?

"You're up early," Ethan's husky voice behind her accused.

Claire turned, smiling guiltily—she hadn't even checked the time, but who could sleep with all that sun filtering in—and nearly fell back against one of the Adirondack chairs when she saw Ethan grinning back at her. He was propped up on one elbow, still in bed, his brown hair tousled this way and that, his grin positively wicked. She swallowed hard as he reached down to scratch his stomach over the tight white T-shirt he wore, and then stretched his arms, yawning dramatically, making the cords of his muscles pull against his skin. Her entire body stiffened as he slowly brought himself up to a sitting position and then reached for the blankets, wondering if she should look away now, before she saw something she shouldn't. Even boxers felt wrong. Wrong! But to her great relief—and strangely, a twinge of disappointment—he was wearing cotton pajama pants in what appeared a considerably more seasonably appropriate material than her own.

"It's warm in here," he said, walking over to stand in the opening to the patio. He slid his gaze up and down her, looking at her as if she were crazy. "You didn't overheat in that granny wear?"

Granny wear! Claire rolled her eyes. More like appropriate attire for hotel air-conditioning, and sharing a bed with your super hot best friend. "Oh, you know me. I'm always cold." Her face felt flush, and for some reason she had the sinking feeling that it had nothing to do with the extra-thick flannel that covered ninety percent of her body. In the early sunlight, Ethan's eyes shone bright, and his chin bore a fresh layer of stubble. He smelled like musk and sleep and—

She rubbed her nose. Certainly no point in going there. The man was practically like a brother to her. Not that she had a brother to compare. Okay, he was like a cousin. Yes, she was as close to him as she was to Hailey.

Except Ethan wasn't a blood relative. But he was still very much off-limits.

"I packed for the hotel. You know how those places

can be, always cranking up the AC," she said, pushing past him into the room to select her outfit from the closet. "I assumed I'd freeze all night."

"Oh, I'd never let you freeze," Ethan said roughly, and her breath caught as she snatched a sundress from its hanger. She turned, heart pounding, to see where he was going with this, but there was a twinkle in his eye when she finally looked his way.

She pursed her lips as he burst out laughing, and despite herself, she joined in. She never could resist that laugh.

It was Ethan's suggestion to cycle into town before the members of the main house awoke, claiming he needed to ease into the day and all it held, and Claire happily agreed. She was eager to see the town and visit some of the shops his mother had mentioned.

They found a pair of old bicycles in the detached garage and set off on the gravel path, Claire trailing Ethan by a few yards, her legs wobbly until she finally got her bearing. Before long, they were approaching the stretch of downtown that Claire had admired when they'd driven through yesterday afternoon. The smells of lilacs and roses filled the air, and birds chirped as they flew from tree to tree. Claire smiled to herself. These were the little things she hadn't appreciated in far too long. She'd been too wrapped up in taxi cabs and subway stops and ambulances flying by. And thinking of Matt, of course.

"I wasn't sure you knew how to ride a bike," he said,

when they finally pulled to a stop in front of a small diner in town.

"Who doesn't know how to ride a bike?" she asked quizzically, tapping at her kickstand. "Just because you've never seen me ride a bike doesn't mean I can't do it."

He shrugged. "True enough. But if you must know, I didn't learn to ride a bike until I was thirteen." He held up a finger, his expression grave. "And if you tell anyone, I will murder you in your sleep with one of those damned towels. I mean that."

Claire stifled her laughter at the ominous lift of his eyebrows and allowed Ethan to hold the restaurant's door open for her. She'd assumed they'd be one of the first customers of the day, but the small establishment was nearly full, leaving them with only a spot at the counter.

"And why is it exactly that you didn't learn to . . . you know," she lowered her voice.

Ethan picked up his menu, studied it, and set it back down again decisively. He stared straight ahead, not looking at her. "My dad was supposed to teach me to ride a bike. After he died, I didn't want to bother my mom with it, and I think she just assumed I knew how. She was so preoccupied with caring for three young kids all on her own. It wasn't until I was thirteen that I figured if I didn't teach myself, I could forget any kind of normal social life until I finally got a driver's license." He tapped his chin. "See that scar? Split my chin wide open the first day out."

"Ouch." Claire frowned a little. "But you kept going."

He shrugged. "What other choice is there?"

Never much of a breakfast eater, Claire ordered a coffee and a blueberry muffin, saying nothing when Ethan opted for the four-egg omelet with extra hash browns and a side of bacon.

"I'm hungry," he said edgily, when the waitress finished pouring their coffee.

"I didn't say anything," she replied. "It's just not like you."

"Yeah, well, being back in the town where you grew up will do that to you. Especially a town like this."

Claire wasn't buying it. "A town with cobblestone streets and iron lampposts and bicycle paths leading back to your lakefront home?"

But Ethan just rubbed at his jaw, his eyes hardening before he looked away. "You wouldn't understand."

It was the first time he'd ever accused her of such a thing, and shame flooded her cheeks with heat. She set her hand on his arm, feeling uneasy at how comfortable it felt there. "Eth, I'm sorry. I was just focused on how tranquil this town is, how beautiful, and quaint. But it's different for you. It holds other meaning. I understand. As much as it hurt when my dad sold my childhood home, the other part of me was relieved." She frowned. It would have been hard, going back, walking from room to room, looking for her mother and never finding her, always being reminded of her absence like that. But at the same time . . . Her chest tightened. She shook her head clear. No use thinking of things that could never be.

He patted her hand, and Claire tensed, wanting to snatch it back, to shift her stool, but as luck would have it they seemed to be bolted to the floor. She fumbled to reach for her coffee mug instead, nearly spilling it all over the Formica surface.

Okay, this had to stop. When had she reacted so strongly to Ethan simply touching her before?

She wasn't so sure she wanted to explore the reason just now. "So what's on the schedule for the day?" she asked, happy to change the subject.

"Oh, I figured we could visit some of the shops this morning, maybe ride around town a bit, grab some lunch. Tonight is party night." His eyelids drooped. "Girls at the house. Men at a pub. You don't have to go, you know."

Claire stirred sugar into her coffee. "Why not? It sounds fun. Besides, a night with the girls is exactly what I need right now, no offense. If I sit alone in that cottage, my mind will just end up wandering."

Ethan frowned. "Still thinking about Matt, then?" His tone was a little harsher than she'd expected, and Claire blinked at him in confusion, wondering where the sudden burst of emotion was coming from.

Ethan raked a hand through his hair, dragging out a sigh. "Sorry. I just . . . I wish you'd get over that jerk."

Claire considered that the same words were probably spoken of him, by friends of the girls whose hearts he had broken, but said nothing. Their food was up, and as she bit into the streusel topped muffin, Claire decided that Ethan was right. There was no reason to be thinking of

Matt.

At least not for today.

*

"Mind if we stop in here?" Claire asked, pointing to a women's clothing boutique that Ethan hadn't noticed before.

He eyed her. "Don't you think you brought enough for a long weekend?"

"It's the pajamas," she admitted, blushing. In the morning sunlight, the hint of pink brought out the blueness of her eyes, giving her a softer, more youthful appearance.

His mouth twitched, but he pushed on the door just the same, telling himself to rein it in. It was fun to mess with Claire, but he needed to be sure it didn't border on flirting. It came easily, maybe even naturally at this point, but with Claire there had to be boundaries.

The sales assistant was busy chatting with other customers, and Ethan followed Claire through the shop, pausing when she did, amused by the way she stopped to admire a red sundress that was hanging on display. She touched the hem, considering the material between her fingers, and then stood back to eye it properly. It wasn't until he cleared his throat that she jumped, turning to face him, her expression the picture of guilt.

"Pajamas," he ordered. "That suitcase will pop if you add anything more to it."

She sighed. "You're right. I was just thinking . . ." She shook her head. "Forget it, I shouldn't have said anything."

He leaned against a nearby side table, growing curious. "Go on. Tell me."

"Well, it's just . . ." She blushed again, and then tucked a strand of hair behind her ear, shaking her head.

"Tell me," he urged, now more curious than ever. It wasn't like Claire to hold anything back from him.

"You won't like it," she warned, and then huffed when he stood patiently waiting. "I was remembering that Matt always liked it when I wore that shade of red. It's very hard to find, and, well . . ."

"You were thinking that if you bought it and somehow ran into him again wearing it that he'd realized he had made a huge mistake and give you the diamond instead of this other woman?"

Claire grimaced. "That obvious?"

He cursed under his breath and moved toward her, setting his hand on her shoulder as he looked her in her eyes. "You're better than this, Claire. And I know you don't believe me, but you will be happier without him. Once you let yourself."

Tears brimmed in her eyes, and he squeezed her shoulder, resisting the urge to pull her in for a hug, to hold her close, smooth her hair, take away the pain. It tore at him to see her like this, over someone so undeserving, someone so . . . wrong. It was just like—

"Ethan? Ethan Parker?"

Ethan dropped his hand and turned to see Marcy McMullen standing at the counter, her brown eyes lit with something he could only call intrigue.

He swept his eyes over the room, and then, breathing a little easier, back to her. "Well, Marcy McMullen. Fancy seeing you here." He flashed her one of his easy grins, but it felt stiff and wary.

"I should be saying the same. Back in town for your cousin's wedding?" She gave him the once-over and skirted her eyes to Claire with noticeable interest.

Suddenly remembering that Claire was standing beside him, he reached over and lightly touched her back. "This is Claire Wells. Claire, Marcy McMullen."

"I recognize your picture from Ethan's yearbook," Claire said pleasantly, reaching out to extend her hand. "You were on the debate team. Or at least in the photo."

Now Marcy's eyes popped with interest, and she looked at him for an explanation. Ethan did his best not to show his impatience. Half the town would get wind of this conversation before noon, no doubt. His pulse kicked at the thought.

"Claire and I were going down memory lane last night. I'm afraid I couldn't hide my past from her forever."

As much as he tried to.

He swallowed uneasily, bracing himself for Marcy's next words, for the question that was on the tip of his tongue, for the name they had in common. The person he didn't like to speak of. The girl he didn't want to discuss.

"Well, it was good seeing you, but I'm afraid we're in a bit of a rush," he explained, hoping that would be the end of that.

"Just here to pick up some pajamas," Claire explained. "I'm afraid the ones I packed weren't appropriate for such warm nights."

Ethan was relieved to see Marcy's demeanor change, and she squared her shoulders and strode purposefully to the back of the room, saying, "We have a wonderful lingerie selection." She picked up something lacy and black, and Ethan felt Claire freeze beside him. Nearly tripping over her heels, he pushed her forward, sensing the resistance of her body against his fingertips that pressed deeper into her lower back.

"Well, actually, I was thinking . . ." Claire's hand extended in the direction of a matronly white cotton pajama set that may as well have had a turtleneck. Ethan's hand shot up and snatched the nearest item off a hanger, thrusting it into her palm.

"Of this?" He grinned, catching the horror in her eyes. "But remember, red is your color, darling."

Her cheeks turned the same shade as the lacy object he was clutching in his hand.

"But remember, *sweetheart*, we're staying at your mother's house." With that, Claire wrestled the flimsy material from his hand and slid it back onto its hanger.

"Oh, well, I suppose that puts a cramp in things." Marcy nodded sagely. "If it's something you can be seen in at the breakfast table that you're looking for, then you'll probably stick with these." She motioned to a rack of cotton pajama pants and shorts and matching T-shirts.

"Why didn't you just pack something like this for the trip?" Ethan wondered aloud, but Claire just shot him a look.

"I told you, I get cold in air-conditioning, and I thought we were staying in a hotel. Besides, the ones I brought certainly came in handy last night, well, aside from the ninety-degree temperature."

Ethan pretended to have serious input on the color and print selections, hoping that Marcy would catch the drift and walk away, but instead she lingered, just in his periphery, making his hands sweat and his heart speed up. *Don't ask. Don't mention anything. Just let it go.*

They managed to get to the counter with only some banal pleasantries about the shop's offerings, and the weather, and the upcoming wedding, of course. The door was so close, it would only take two long strides to get through it, to be back on the street, to be free.

"My own cousin is getting married this weekend, too," Marcy said, smiling. "Should be quite a weekend for us both."

Ethan nodded, muttering something under his breath that showed he had heard, and turned to look out the window. The shops were opening, one by one, and people filled the sidewalks, sipping coffee in paper cups, wearing straw hats to block the sun. Weekends were always a busy time in Grey Harbor, with the tourists flocking from May through August. He supposed he was one of them himself now. There had been so much turnover since he'd last been here, and even more the time before. Life was changing, moving forward, so why was it that when he came back here, he always felt stuck in the past?

The women were talking about clothes and wedding reception dresses now, a safe subject, Ethan was pleased to note, but as Marcy handed over the paper bag containing Claire's new, boring pajamas, she met his eye, and Ethan just knew, the way he always knew when the subject would be broached, because his sensitivity was on high, always on alert, the few times he dared to return.

"You'll never guess who else is in town this weekend!" Marcy had a distinctive glint in her eyes.

His gritted his teeth, willing her to stop, but it was too late, the seed was planted, the notion formed, and the realization a cold grip on his heart.

Of all the dumb luck.

"Kimberly Listner." She watched him carefully, gauging his reaction, and Ethan was careful to give none.

"What a coincidence," he said. "I'll keep an eye out for her then." He'd do no such thing. "Claire," he said, already moving toward the door, hoping she didn't see the strain in his face and question him about it. "Shall we?"

Claire thanked Marcy and followed him to the door, and it wasn't until the door was firmly closed behind them that Ethan felt his shoulders relax.

"Was that an old school friend?" Claire asked mildly, as they walked down the street.

Ethan kept his eyes straight ahead, afraid of what he would see if he looked anywhere else. "Something like that."

Chapter Seven

"Do I smell a cigarette?" Barbara sniffed the air, frowning. "I *told* Amelia not to smoke within twenty feet of this house." She put more force into whipping the cream. Claire frowned as the liquid turned to soft peaks, remembering the way she and her mother would do the same thing each Christmas, when they made their annual trifle dessert.

She blinked and looked away before the tears could form. She missed her mother, but she was ashamed to realize she didn't think of her as often as she should anymore. Not daily, at least, and not with the same pain that seemed to linger forever in those early months. Now, being here, in a family home, with so much love and laughter and even arguing, she couldn't help but think of the old days, and a little part of her tore open again when she realized they were over.

Still, she thought, watching Ethan's mother whip and stir and refer to her list of hors d'oeuvres, it was nice to remember those days, too. Nice to be reminded.

And nice to be here, she realized, feeling that twinge of guilt resurface. Ethan's family may have their quirks, but there was something warm and familiar about that. Much like Ethan himself.

Barbara set down her whisk and sniffed again. She walked over to the window above the sink and clucked her tongue. "Yep. Thought so. Cigarettes. She knows how I feel about that."

"I thought she quit," remarked Milly, who had stopped into the kitchen to refill her glass of Chardonnay.

"Oh, she did, and I'm sure she will again, but you know how these things can be." She gave Claire a wince as she moved the bowl to the side of the counter. "Weddings. They're difficult for the broken-hearted."

You could say that again, thought Claire. She finished slicing one of the baguettes Barbara had warmed in the oven and arranged it on a cheese board, trying not to let herself think of Matt, or the woman he'd left her for. Was the ring still hidden away, in a coat pocket, or in a drawer? Or had he already proposed, already promised himself to some lucky, faceless woman by the vaguely referenced name of Heather, who Claire could never compare to?

She swallowed the lump in her throat and moved on to the second baguette.

She'd started dating Matt just before her mother had died. He hadn't come to her funeral; Ethan had instead. It didn't seem right, bringing Matt, when he was still a new and exciting and uncertain feature in her life. Ethan had driven her the six hours to her childhood home, with Hailey in the backseat, brought her cups of tea, and picked up dinner for her father and aunt each night. Hailey had stayed close, sharing her double bed the way they had when they were little, enjoying "princess sleepovers" where they giggled in the dark long after they were supposed to be asleep. Ethan slept on a pull-out couch in the basement's rec room, but somehow, knowing he was there, two levels below, brought her some sense of peace.

Ethan had never met her mother, but somehow, she always felt he had in a way.

Matt had never asked much about her, and she hadn't dwelled on the subject, saving that instead for those closest to her, separate from a budding romance.

Claire blinked. When had Matt become the person closest to her, then? Or had he never done so? Had she read it all wrong?

"Everything okay, hon?" Barbara set a hand on her wrist. Her green eyes were soft, much like Ethan's, when Claire looked up, giving a brave smile.

She brushed a strand of hair from her cheek with the back of her hand. "Never better. In fact, I was just thinking that it's been a long time since I've been in a house with so many family members under one roof. I've missed it."

"Are you like Ethan in that you don't get home much?" Barbara shook her head. "You young people are so busy."

"St. Louis was home to me, but my father moved south about a year and a half ago, so it's not the same." *For so many reasons*, Claire thought, thinking of her childhood bedroom that her mother had stenciled on rainy day with yellow daisies, the bookshelf stacked with her dog-eared favorites, the toy box filled with joyful memories, now locked away in a storage unit.

"Do you have any family in Chicago?"

Claire nodded. "My cousin. I'm staying with her for the time being. I'm between jobs at the moment," she explained, wondering if she should have mentioned that part, or if she'd unwittingly put a crack in Ethan's well-crafted façade.

"Well, Ethan says you're very talented. He's been singing your praises." She winked, and for some reason, Claire felt herself blush.

Nonsense, she told herself firmly, reaching for the serrated knife and the cutting board. He was talking her up, adding to his fictitious story. It didn't mean anything beyond that.

"Did you have a nice time in town this morning?" Barbara asked as she refilled the ice bucket.

"I did," Claire said, frowning slightly when she thought of the change in Ethan's demeanor after they'd left the clothing boutique. They'd gone to a few more antique shops, but Ethan didn't seem to stop looking over his shoulder until he was back on the bike, peddling away from town. "Ethan showed me where he went to school. And the park." That's where they'd had lunch, eating sandwiches on a wooden bench, Ethan quieter than usual.

"He loved feeding those ducks when he was young." Barbara's smile turned wistful. "I can still remember the way his little face would fall when he'd get to the last piece of bread in the bag." She laughed and slid on an oven mitt to pull a casserole bowl of crab and artichoke dip from the top rack. She closed the door with her hip, and carefully set the hot dish on an iron trivet. "Of course, that was a long time ago," she added softly.

Claire noticed Barbara's hands were shaking as she opened the top drawer to reach for a serving spoon. She searched her face, sensing that something was amiss, that there was more below the surface than anyone was letting on. Including Ethan.

"Your town is lovely," Claire offered. "I love the cobblestone streets and the architecture. It's small, but so quaint. I have to say that it's nice to get out of the city," she admitted, sighing.

"You know you're always welcome to visit," Barbara said hopefully.

Claire nodded and chewed her lip, remembering again that Ethan's mother thought she was his girlfriend, that they were a couple, a package deal. In many ways they were, but not in the way Barbara so clearly hoped.

Once again, she couldn't help thinking it would have been so much better to have never lied, to have come to Door County as they were—friends—and as they would remain.

A sudden image of Ethan in bed that morning flashed in her mind, and Claire blinked, pushing it back firmly as she added a sprig of grapes to the cheese platter and carried it into the living room, where all the other women were gathered.

"Not exactly a wild night, but I'm too old for that kind of thing," remarked the bride, who couldn't have been much older than Claire.

"What are the guys up to?" one of the older women asked, and Leslie snorted.

"Hitting the bars in town, of course," she remarked and frowned at her carbonated grape juice before forcing a sip.

"Do you know if it's a boy or a girl yet?" Claire asked, taking the seat beside her on the couch.

"We're keeping it a surprise," Leslie replied. "But it would be nice to have another boy in the family to help balance things out."

Claire laughed. Poor Ethan. Growing up in a house full of women couldn't have been easy, but then she supposed it was . . . eye-opening. No wonder he wasn't looking to settle down any time soon. He already had all the women he needed as permanent fixtures. Could she really blame him?

No. But she could worry about him. Especially with how distant he seemed today, how unhappy really. He hadn't even wanted to go out with the guys tonight, and normally he'd love that type of thing. It wasn't like Ethan to sit at home. Ethan liked to be on the go, on the move. Ethan didn't stay still. He just kept moving forward.

She supposed she could learn a thing or two from him.

"So, Claire," Barbara said, balancing her appetizer plate on her knees. "Tell us more about you. What do you and Ethan like to do in the city?"

This one was easy, Claire thought. "Oh, we go to movies, out for drinks. There's this great wine bar we discovered a few—" She'd been about to say years. She licked her lips, and continued. "A few months ago. And we have our favorite restaurants." She shrugged. "Of course, with Ethan's job, he always gets the best reservations."

Milly clucked her tongue. "He gets paid to party!"

"It's not like that," Claire clarified. "The magazine he writes for is really reputable. His column is one that most people read weekly. I know I do."

"Well," Barbara sighed. "It certainly is an interesting subject matter. Bars. Clubs. Concerts."

"And restaurants," Claire pointed out. She didn't bother mentioning that someone else covered musical concerts for the magazine.

"I suppose it suits him," Barbara remarked, seeming a little unconvinced. "It's a good job for when you're young, but when he settles down . . ."

"*If* he settles down," Amelia cried as she waltzed into the room and settled onto a loveseat.

Claire smiled uneasily. "Sometimes we just hang out at home and watch television. Boring stuff."

"Fascinating," Leslie said, her expression one of pure intrigue. Claire glanced self-consciously around the room. Sure enough, heads tipped in thought as they stared at her, as if waiting for her to say something more.

"And do you spend the night at his home?" Milly asked, pursing her lips like a little bird.

Claire's heart began to drum as the heat rose in her cheeks, and she wrestled with what to say, what would be the realistic answer to such a probing question, when Amelia shot her aunt a look of scorn and cried, "Aunt Milly! This is Ethan we're talking about!"

"Yes, but I didn't know if it was different, what with Claire being his actual girlfriend and all. I may be old, but I'm not naïve, dear. For all we know, they're living together!"

A simultaneous gasp went up around the room and all eyes stared at her. The silence crackled as Claire gripped her wine glass until she feared it might shatter in her hands.

"No," she finally said, happy to be honest. "We don't live together." She didn't mention that she'd considered it, though, given her current living situation and all.

She frowned, thinking of the call from Hailey she still hadn't returned. It was easier to avoid her somehow, until she'd figured out what she was going to do. Or what she was going to say when they eventually talked.

"You must excuse the interrogation," Barbara said, giving her a conspiratorial smile. "It's just that Ethan hasn't dated anyone seriously in so long."

So long? Claire frowned.

"No," Milly added sagely. "Not since—"

Barbara cleared her throat, and Milly reddened a bit in the cheeks before immediately cramming her mouth with a mini quiche.

"Let's just say that Ethan hasn't brought anyone home in a while," Leslie said mildly.

"There's more to life than dating," Amelia said a little hostilely.

"I'm so thrilled to hear you say that!" Barbara beamed, and Amelia shot her an angry look.

"Yes, what is it that you do again, Amelia?" Claire asked, eager to interfere at the slightest hint of conflict that seemed to keep brewing to the surface.

"Oh, I'm between jobs at the moment," Amelia said, skirting her eyes to the left.

The room fell silent, and Claire feared she had touched upon yet another touchy subject. She reached for her wine, taking a small sip because she felt the need to keep her wits about her, lest she slip and admit that she and Ethan weren't actually, technically, madly in love. Perhaps she should hint that there was trouble in paradise so that they all wouldn't be so shocked when things ended? Or perhaps, given Ethan's track record, they already saw her fate, before Claire, well, *girlfriend* Claire, saw it for herself.

She suddenly felt a little sorry for the fake Claire, sitting here, meeting her boyfriend's family for the first time, somehow none the wiser that her beloved boyfriend was known to play the field and that she didn't really stand a chance.

She frowned. That fake Claire felt an awful lot like real Claire. When she'd been with Matt.

"It takes time to meet that special someone," one of the younger cousins encouraged, and Amelia gave a derisive snort in return.

Before anyone else could say something, Amelia stood up and left the room through the back screen door, leaving the rest of the room in silence. Barbara reached for her glass of wine, shaking her head in dismay.

"I'd run after her, but I don't think that's what she wants," she said sadly. "She needs to sort this through on her own."

"Still not over Will, I see," remarked Milly, as she wedged a piece of cheddar into her mouth.

"Some people aren't easy to forget, I suppose. But I do wish she'd take after her brother and move on," Barbara said, casting a glance in Claire's direction.

Claire reached for her wine glass and pretended not to have heard the comment as she discussed potential baby names with Leslie, who was all too happy to share her thoughts on the subject. But as she listened to Ethan's sister go through her list, struggling over recent popularity versus tradition, Claire couldn't help but keep an ear out for Barbara's conversation, and she wondered, more than idly, just what she had meant when she said that Ethan had moved on.

From whom?

*

Ethan stared into his beer, happy that a noisy pub had been chosen for tonight's festivities. The last thing he wanted to do was sit and talk. Besides, there was no way Kimberly would come into this place. She hated it. Always had.

He was safe here. So really, he needed to stop looking over his shoulder every ten minutes.

He took a long pull on his beer and flagged the waiter for another. His cousins and their friends were already rowdy, shooting pool, tossing darts, commenting on the baseball game that was playing on the television. He knew he should join in, shake himself out of this funk, because that's all it was, a funk.

He cursed under his breath. He was behaving like Claire, going against his own advice. He was a hypocrite. But damn it if he couldn't help it.

He knew what he said. He knew how he came across. A flirt. A cad. A womanizer. But that wasn't who he was, not deep down, at least. Even though he tried, and oh, how he'd tried. To move on, to not look back, to never let it happen again.

"Love," he snorted aloud. "Who needs it?"

"Don't let Eddie hear you say that," his cousin Dominic said, sliding next to him. "Have you seen the man tonight? Looks like he's just seen a ghost!" He chuckled ruefully as he brought the beer to his lips.

Ethan looked over his shoulder where Eddie was shooting pool. Sure enough, the man's eyes looked a little glazed, and there was a confused frown to his forehead.

"Marriage. Who needs it," Ethan said, turning back to the game.

"Don't let your girlfriend hear you say that!" his cousin Rob called from the corner of the bar.

"Don't you worry about Claire," Ethan said, hiding a smile. But it was true. If Claire were his girlfriend, she'd be expecting the picket fence, the kid, the yard. Things he couldn't offer. Or maybe just things he no longer believed in.

He frowned. Best to remember that.

"Aw, now, you can't fool me, Eth. We all know how you feel about marriage." Dominic gave him a knowing smirk, and Ethan felt his back teeth graze.

"What? I hit a nerve? You know Kimberly's in town this weekend—"

"Don't go there," Ethan said acidly, taking another long sip of his drink.

"Hey, if you're still hung up on her, I'll take Claire," called Rob, giving a wolfish grin.

Ethan shot him a hard look. "Cut it out," he snapped.

"I'm just saying, she's pretty easy on the eye. Nice ass,

too."

"I'm warning you. Don't speak about her like that," Ethan hissed. His breath turned ragged as his anger burned.

"Hey, he's just a little drunk. Cut him some slack," Rob's brother, Ted, said, coming to set another round on the table. "Since when did you all get all sensitive on us?"

"I just don't like him speaking about Claire that way. Got it?"

"Whoa," Rob said, laughing until the beer sputtered from his mouth. "You've got it bad."

"I do not have it bad. I just don't like you talking about her that way, okay?" Fire heated his blood and Ethan took a sip of beer to cool his anger. Ted was right. Rob was drunk. He should call it a night. Go home.

He pulled out his wallet and set a bill on the table to cover his share and a few rounds for everyone else. Tipping his head to swallow the dregs in his glass, he pushed back his chair and stood. "It's been real, gentlemen, but I'm heading out."

"Already? But the girls haven't even arrived," Rob said, and Ethan just narrowed his eyes. They all knew what Rob meant by "girls."

"Good night," he said, turning to go.

"Heading home to his lady," Rob cried, laughing.

Ethan stopped, knowing he should let it drop, but he couldn't. "And what are you heading home to?" he asked, raising an eyebrow.

"I don't know," said Rob. "Now that Kimberly's back

in town, I might head over to one of the other bars, see if she's around. You wouldn't mind, would you, Eth?"

Ethan ground on his teeth, holding the challenge in his cousin's gaze, telling himself not to feed it. Rob had always been this way with him—rumor was he'd been sweet on Kimberly back in high school. From the looks of it, he was still hell-bent on punishing Ethan for it.

Ethan's hand felt balmy as he pulled it into a fist at his side, wondering which of the comments he was more worked up about. The ones about Claire, or the ones about Kimberly.

"Wouldn't mind at all," he said tightly. He walked to the door and pushed out into the cool night air, and began the walk back to the house, not pausing to look back.

*

Claire was in the kitchen when Ethan came through the screen door; his shoulders hunched a little as he stepped inside.

The party had died down forty minutes ago, with the bride claiming she needed her beauty sleep, and her sisters and friends following suit. The older women seemed happy to be relieved of the event, immediately claiming they were off too, leaving Claire, Amelia, and Barbara to clean up—it had only seemed fair to send Leslie up to bed.

"I saw the light on," Ethan said, opening the fridge

and reaching for a bottle of water. He gave her a quizzical look. "Is everyone else asleep?"

"Well, it is eleven thirty. Though, Amelia did mention something about seeing what was going on in town," she said, raising an eyebrow.

"Meaning *who's* in town." Ethan shook his head. "It's been almost a year since the breakup and she's still hoping he'll have a change of heart."

Claire frowned at that. She couldn't exactly fault Amelia. Hope was a powerful thing.

But then, so was denial.

She realized, with a jolt, that while Amelia maybe still had something to cling to, she did not. Not when Matt was proposing to another woman. She was free, but he was not. And that, well, that was closure, wasn't it?

"Do you think she'll find what she's looking for?" Claire suddenly felt defensive of Amelia. She may have tired the patience of her family members, but there was something romantic about unrequited love.

And that was officially crazy talk. She opened the fridge and took a bottle of water out for herself. Time to clear her head.

"Do any of us find what we're looking for?" Ethan asked mildly, coming to stand next to her at the breakfast bar.

Claire shrugged. Once she would have said so, but now . . . "I don't know. I suppose that's what life is all about, though, isn't it? The belief that somehow, someway, it will all work out for us in the end?"

She blinked quickly, but it was too late. The tears were there, burning the back of her eyes, threatening to spill. She was just tired, worn out, and worried. Hailey had called again, and Claire knew she couldn't dodge her forever.

Ethan frowned and set both hands on her shoulders, looking her in the eyes. "Promise me, Claire. Promise me you will not turn into Amelia. Promise me you will move on, live your life."

Claire nodded in amusement, deciding that Ethan had definitely enjoyed a few beers this evening. She held up two fingers and sniffed. "Scout's honor."

"I mean it, Claire," Ethan said, his face serious, his eyes earnest. He lifted one hand from her shoulder to brush a strand of hair from her cheek, his gaze unwavering. "You have too much to offer. Too much going for you. I want to see you happy again."

"I am happy," she assured him. She blinked, struggling to maintain eye contact. His gaze was too intense, and his thumb, it was still lingering on her skin, caressing her cheek.

His eyes drifted lower, to her mouth, and Claire felt her breath catch as the silence between them stretched. She shivered.

"Cold?" He arched an eyebrow; a look he did well.

She nodded, seizing her chance to pull away, to create some distance between herself and . . . whatever this was. She closed the kitchen door, but only a little. She would go back to the boathouse, take a shower, or go to bed.

"I might need those flannel pajamas after all," she joked, and then stiffened, realizing the truth in her words.

Ethan was still standing near the counter, his expression pensive, his smile a little wan. "I think I'll stick around here for a bit until I get tired."

Claire nodded. "Great," she said, even as she registered that little tug of disappointment in her chest. She smiled tightly as she slipped through the door, wondering what had just happened back there, and what might have happened if she'd stayed.

Chapter Eight

Ethan wasn't in bed when Claire woke up the next morning, her skin cool and her head a little foggy. She blinked into the sunshine that filtered through the French doors, and then startled all at once when she remembered last night, the strange impasse between them, the way Ethan had held her gaze a little too long, his eyes drifting dangerously to her lips.

He'd had too much to drink at the bachelor party, she decided. That explained it. Except that he didn't seem all that drunk, really, and she'd been out with him for drinks hundreds of times before and never, ever had he looked at her that way before.

She pulled in a breath and blew it out quickly. She was overthinking this, imagining things that weren't there. After all, nothing had happened. He hadn't made a move on her. He'd respectfully stayed on his side of the rolled up towels.

Except. . . She frowned, staring at the perfectly smooth pillow and sheets on his side of the bed. On second look, Ethan hadn't come to bed at all.

She studied the empty space where his body should have been, and then, for reasons she couldn't explain and certainly couldn't justify, bent down to sniff his pillow. She closed her eyes, locking in the musky scent, and then, just as quickly, snapped her eyes open and jumped out of bed. She was lonely. Clearly, very, very lonely, and very, very desperate.

She was better than this, as Ethan would say. After all, if she described a man exactly like him, to him, he would instruct her to run for the hills.

Or maybe to relax and have a little fun.

But he never, ever, ever would have told her to fall for him. She frowned at herself. Of course not! He was her friend—her dearest, closest friend. The man who wiped away tears and made her laugh and was always there, her rock. Ethan may be loyal to her, but he was hardly that way with the women he saw in a . . . *sexual* light. She couldn't start thinking of him in *that* way. That would . . . Well, that would just ruin everything.

She showered and changed quickly, ready for another day exploring Ethan's quaint hometown. Today he had said they would have lunch on the pier, and from the looks of the still waters sparkling under the morning sun, it was the perfect weather for it.

She had barely pushed through the front door of the cottage when she spotted Ethan lying in the hammock, his feet crossed, his arms resting on his stomach. She stopped walking, eyeing him suspiciously, and, curious, ventured closer across the cool green lawn, still damp with dew.

He roused as she approached, the twig she accidentally broke under her sandaled feet snapping him from his slumber. Claire took in last night's clothes and the dazed look in his eyes and started laughing. "You *slept* out here?"

He rubbed a hand over his face and looked around. "Wouldn't be the first time. Although last time I wasn't alone." He gave a wolfish grin, and Claire rolled her eyes.

See, Claire? Cute, dependable. And all wrong.

"I just assumed you'd crashed in the house," she said, stepping back to give him room to slide off the hammock.

"And give them reason to speculate?" Ethan cocked an eyebrow. "I should probably go freshen up before they see me. If they haven't already," he added darkly. He glanced warily toward the house, cupping a hand over his eyes to shield the sun.

"I'll wait outside for you," Claire said, deciding she might like the chance to sit on one of those Adirondack chairs and look out at the water for a bit. They went back into the cottage, Ethan turning toward the bathroom while Claire walked around the structure to the small patio, stopping to admire the rose bushes Barbara was so proud of. The water was so close, she could almost hear it lapping gently at the shore, and seagulls swooped down, casting shadows on the blue surface.

She settled onto a chair and rested her head back. They had a beach in Chicago, of course, but it was crowded, full of people sunbathing and playing volleyball; it was nothing like this. Here she could think, clear her head, think about the future.

But for some reason, right now, all she wanted to do was to focus on the present. She had all the time in the world to worry about tomorrow, and she was rather looking forward to today.

She snorted to herself. When was the last time she'd thought that?

The day she and Matt had been planning to move to California, that's when. She'd been so full of hope then, so full of anticipation. But she'd also been so full of another thing. Something she hadn't wanted to admit to herself at the time. Something she'd tried not to think about, something she'd told herself was silly and out of place.

Something that felt an awful lot like doubt.

She could still pinpoint the exact moment she'd felt it. It wasn't when she'd told Hailey; no, her cousin had been too busy popping the champagne and squealing for all the details. It hadn't been when she'd given notice at the auction house, either; though she loved her job, she'd been there since she was twenty-two and was ready for a new challenge.

It had been when she'd told Ethan. She'd assumed he'd have the same reaction as Hailey, that he'd buy a round of drinks, talk about annual visits to Wine Country, or, that, being Ethan, he'd roll his eyes and say she was too young to settle down, but, of course, if one must, a fabulous West Coast lifestyle was the way to go.

Instead, he'd said nothing at all. He'd just looked at her strangely, and finally, after what felt like the longest silence of their friendship, had simply said, "If that's what you want, then I'm happy for you."

Only he didn't seem happy. She told herself it couldn't have been about Matt—they got along just fine. But that night, after she went back to her apartment, the apartment she would soon be leaving, even though she loved that apartment, with its tall windows and its short walk to the "L" station, she felt as if someone had come along and popped the dream she'd been building up all week. She'd imagined it all—she and Matt on the beach, taking tours of the vineyards, sitting on a patio, the sunshine in their faces, eating fresh vegetables and buying a juicer. She saw open windows, curtains billowing, white furniture and sea blue walls. But those images became harder to cling to as the doubt crept in. And soon she found herself shopping for her new lifestyle, focusing on the petty necessitates like rugs and color schemes, anything to maintain the joy she had felt at the first promise of this next step.

It was change. A good change. But something else had changed, too. She and Ethan were inseparable; even when they were dating other people, they still made time for each other, and she still laughed harder with Ethan than she ever had with Matt. And that, she knew, was troubling.

And when she went to California, there would be no hours-long chats over a shared bottle of wine, no last-minute excursions to see the latest Woody Allen movie, no lazy nights watching crappy reality television. There would just be Matt. And for some reason, that didn't feel like enough.

Claire bent down and picked up a rock, rubbing her thumb against the smooth grain before tossing it into the lake. She'd forgotten to flick her wrist, and the stone dropped heavily into the water, sinking to the bottom in a hopeless way, as if it had had a chance of making more of its situation and now that opportunity was gone.

Claire thought back to last night, wondering what might have happened if she hadn't stepped back from Ethan's gaze, hadn't listened so firmly to her head and kept him just out of reach. Would Ethan have kissed her last night?

And would she have let him?

She hadn't dared to think of it, to imagine what it might be like, not just to kiss him, but to make this something real, something permanent, to finish what they'd started. A foundation. A relationship. A bond.

"Penny for your thoughts," a deep voice behind her

rumbled, and Claire jumped, turning to flash Ethan a guilty smile.

He was dressed, but his hair was still damp and tousled and anything she'd seen in his eyes last night had vanished, replaced with the Ethan she knew back in Chicago, with a hint of a smirk on his mouth and a slightly amused glint to his eyes. He came out onto the patio, walking as casually as always, and picked up a stone. It skipped effortlessly across the water, making at least four stops before disappearing into the dark water. Ethan looked at her, his expression deadpan. "Last one to the bike shed buys lunch."

And he was off, running ahead of her at full speed, not willing to let her win, or maybe, not willing to let her ever catch him.

She couldn't be sure anymore.

*

Ethan pushed his toes into the sand and looked out onto the water, where sail masts caught the wind, moving like small white dots across the horizon. Claire was standing at the edge, gingerly dipping her feet in what he knew to be icy water. She glanced over her shoulder, tossing him a grin.

"I was hoping it would be warmer up here," she said.

"In Wisconsin? We're farther north, not south. Same lake. Same water."

"Wishful thinking." She shrugged, then turned back to

the water. Her long blonde hair billowed in the breeze, and the hem of her dress bounced against the back of her knees, dragging his attention to her long, smooth legs.

He sucked in a breath, counted to five, told himself to quit it, to cool down, to stop getting caught up in the moment. Claire was pretty, but lots of girls were. Didn't mean he had to go there.

He bent his legs, roping his arms over his knees, his eyes trained on the sand. He was getting sentimental, emotional. He wasn't thinking clearly. He never did when he was back here. There were too many memories that muddled his head.

Everything would be back to normal when he was back in Chicago. If he could, he'd get in the car and leave right now.

He looked up at Claire as she came walking toward him now, her stride slow as she maneuvered through the thick sand. His jaw tensed. For a moment, the distractions of the city were the last thing on his mind. And this . . . the beach, the sand, the soft sounds of the water, and that smile . . . It was enough to keep him here forever.

"I like this little beach," Claire said as she dropped onto the sand beside him, her hair skimming his arm, sending a rush of heat through his blood. "It's quiet. Doesn't seem like many people come here."

"A group of us used to come here back on college breaks," he mused, remembering the bonfires that started long before sunset, the way the sun turned from blue to orange and then faded to black, making it impossible to know where the sand ended and the water began.

"Your mom implied that you never come back to Grey Harbor anymore," Claire remarked. "And when I think about it, your sister's wedding last summer was the only time I could think of that you've been here in the three years since we've known each other."

"It's not the same coming here anymore," he said, resting his elbows on his knees. "It makes me think about the past. You know I don't like thinking about the past."

"It's one thing to dwell on the past," Claire pointed out. "But I suppose I'm guilty of it, too. Last night when I was hanging out with your mom in the kitchen, it made me think of these desserts my mother and I would always make for the holidays. I'd nearly forgotten that memory. It shook me up."

"You'll never forget your mother," Ethan said firmly.

Her head was down and she was drawing a pattern in the sand with a stick, tracing loops and then smoothing it out with her palm. She shrugged. "I'll never forget her, but all those little things that felt so ordinary at the time; I don't want to lose that. I want to remember. Even if it hurts to think of her, to know she's gone, I want to hold on."

Ethan looked back at the water. "I guess it's easy sometimes not to think about the past."

Claire grew quiet for a moment. "Matt was a good distraction for me. We had just met, and . . . you know how it is. That first flush when you meet someone new. Everything feels exciting."

Oh, he knew how it was. He'd built his life around that rush, never lingering long enough for it to fade. "Don't beat yourself up. You were coping."

"I was hiding," she corrected. She shook her head. "I didn't talk about my mom with Matt. I guess I got caught up in the escape instead. Sometimes I wonder what was real with Matt and what wasn't anymore."

"Sometimes avoidance helps. When I'm away from here, it's easier."

"You miss your father," Claire observed. Her eyes drifted over his face. A strand of hair caught her cheek and she pushed it back before he could reach for it.

"He used to take me fishing, over at that pond in the park we were at yesterday." Ethan smiled sadly. "They stock the pond. I didn't know it at the time. I just knew that every time we went out we always caught something. Always threw it back." His gut hurt when he thought of the way his dad had feigned surprise every time Ethan triumphantly reeled one in.

"You know I never brought anyone to that pond before." He frowned, wondering why he'd stayed away so long. Why he suddenly felt okay going back. He could have brought Kimberly, a hundred times. But he hadn't wanted to share that with her. It had been easier to get lost in her, in what they shared.

Like Claire and Matt, he supposed.

"Your mother is so happy to have you home. I'm sure

it helps her, too, having you back." Claire's tone was gentle, but he understood what she was saying. He needed to set his feelings aside, needed to remind himself that he wasn't the only one that had lost someone. She was right.

"Grey Harbor holds a lot of memories, not just of my dad. I dated a girl from here for a while. Guess I started staying away after that."

Claire blinked at him, her eyes going wide. "You *dated* a girl? As in, more than one date? You. Lothario. Don Juan. Confirmed bachelor."

Despite himself, he grinned. "Kimberly." He didn't like saying her name. "We met in high school, went to the same college. Came back here together for every holiday, every summer. I even thought about marrying her." He shook his head. Seemed like a million years ago, and yet, in many ways it felt like yesterday.

"What happened?" Claire asked, her eyes sharp on his.

He shrugged, looked out onto the water. "It ended. We were young. We wanted different things, I suppose."

"You loved her," Claire commented, her voice filled with wonder. When he said nothing, she swatted his arm. "You loved her," she said again, her tone one of both surprise and accusation. "Ethan Parker. I knew you had it in you." She chuckled, and Ethan jabbed her lightly with his elbow.

"I never said I didn't have it in me." His gaze held hers for a beat, and she finally looked away. "Come on," he said, standing to hold out a hand. "We have that rehearsal dinner to get to. And if my prediction is accurate, we might be taking center stage instead of the bride and groom."

"Don't let the bride hear you say that," Claire laughed, taking his hand to let him pull her up. It felt small in his palm, warm and feminine and . . . right. She stumbled on an uneven patch of sand, and Ethan tightened his grip on her and reached out with the other hand to square her at the hip. "Thanks," she said, fumbling to right herself.

She looked up into his eyes, her gaze questioning. He knew he should release her, step back, fall into their well-established pattern. The one that was so comforting. So easy. So reliable.

Her lips parted slightly, and his chest tightened. It would be so simple to lean in, brush his mouth to hers, press her body against his chest, and make her his.

He blinked, thinking of Kimberly, of how natural that had once felt, and how empty his life had been when she was no longer a part of it. He couldn't stand to think of that happening with Claire. And since they were only friends, he wouldn't have to.

Technically.

He'd come close to losing her once before, when she'd found Matt and started talking about moving to California. Who was to say the same thing wouldn't happen again? A girl like Claire, so sweet, so pretty, so . . . perfect really, wouldn't stay single for long, even if she feared so.

His breath was hard and sharp and he realized he was considering it, kissing her, for the second time in two days. He had the chance to try, to take their friendship to a new level. But he could throw away everything they had in the process.

He pulled back sharply, managing a casual grin. "Don't go doing that with heels on tonight," he warned, and even though she shook her head and tossed him a smile, and even though things were already fading back to normal as they climbed the dunes and padded barefoot onto the wooden path that would lead them back to their bikes, he couldn't stop thinking that the moment was lost, and that if he didn't act fast, didn't stand up and do something, he might lose her forever.

He glanced at her sidelong as she climbed onto her bike seat and pulled her hair up into a ponytail. Who was he kidding? He might lose her anyway. And that . . . well, that was scary.

*

The rehearsal dinner was held at an Italian restaurant in town. Claire noticed that it was a much smaller event than last night's lakeside soiree, and there wouldn't be much chance of breaking away early, unless they wanted everyone to notice their absence and comment on it later.

Since the meal had ended twenty minutes ago, she'd been locked in a conversation with the bride's sister, who was wondering how she might get the attention of one of the more attractive waiters.

"Why don't you just go up to him and say hello?" Claire finally asked, even though she would never be capable of something so daring herself.

Beatrice blanched. "Oh, no. No. I need to find a way to make him come to me, you see. I'm old fashioned that way."

Claire understood. It had never sat right with her that she'd technically spoken to Matt first. He'd been sitting in a crowded coffee shop, reading a newspaper, and she was desperate for a place to sit. She had the choice of asking to share with the safe, nice-looking, elderly woman near the window, or Matt.

Sometimes she wondered how different her path might have been had she chosen not to take a risk that day, not to do something bold and slightly out of character. Careful Claire wouldn't have ended up broken hearted and alone.

"Maybe you could accidentally bump into him," she suggested, and Beatrice chewed her lip in thought.

"What are you ladies canoodling about?" Ethan asked, handing them each a fresh glass of wine. He casually wrapped his hand around Claire's waist, and she felt her breath catch for a moment until she remembered. Girlfriend. Of course.

"Your cousin is trying to get the attention of that waiter over there," Claire whispered, using her eyes to indicate the man in question.

"Tell me, Ethan, what does it take? What makes you

approach a woman?" Beatrice tipped her head, and then remembering Claire was there, turned a little pink in the cheeks. "I mean, it's just . . . Well, Ethan is very lucky with the ladies." She gave an apologetic smile.

Claire waved away her concern. "Oh, I know. I know everything there is to know about this man. Isn't that right, honey?" She craned her neck, looking up to give him a knowing smile, but he seemed thoughtful rather than amused.

"I can still remember the first time I saw Claire. We met playing tennis. She showed up in this little white tennis skirt with her blond ponytail swinging, and everyone else was wearing T-shirts and shorts, and I just remember thinking, I have got to talk to this girl. She played terribly," he said, grinning at her devilishly. "Can't serve to save her life. Still can't. But the way she ran for that ball . . ." He closed his eyes and shook his head, his mouth curving into a slow grin. "It was the worst set I've ever played, and I didn't even care. After, a bunch of us went out for drinks. I couldn't even tell you who else was there. Claire and I talked for four hours, and at the end of the night . . . Well, I just knew that life would never be the same again, and that I had met someone very special."

Without her noticing, a crowd had gathered to listen to the story, and as he leaned over to peck a kiss on her cheek, Claire heard a collective sigh go up in the group. Claire swallowed, feeling shaky and out of sorts; her head was spinning.

It was true. Every word of it was true. They had met playing tennis, something arranged by Hailey who was friends with someone at Ethan's work. And she had worn a white tennis skirt. She hadn't stopped to think he'd noticed. That he'd ever looked at her . . . in that way. And they *had* talked for four hours. She'd assumed it was because they had been seated next to each other, and the bar was loud.

But now, now she wondered if she'd seen it all slightly differently, if maybe there was something more to it, a possibility she hadn't considered, a connection that might have been something more.

Oh, she'd noticed him, of course. Who wouldn't? He was handsome, what with that dark hair and that teasing grin, and that laugh. Oh, that laugh. She never tired of that sound. They'd gone to the bar and they'd talked and laughed, and sure a little part of her was thinking, isn't this perfect? Isn't this the start of something? But more than that, all she could think of was how easy it was to talk to him, as if she'd found the male version of herself, her other half, as if they'd known each other all along, or grown up in a parallel universe, something that made the connection so instantaneous, so easy.

When Hailey had mentioned afterward that he was known to be a flirt, rarely settling down for even a month at a time with a woman, she hadn't felt let down or challenged the way some women might. And when they'd all met up as a group again, for volleyball this time, she just assumed they'd be friends, and she didn't think twice when she pulled a stool up to him at the bar afterward and continued right where they'd left off, eventually making plans for a movie that weekend.

And they'd gone to see it. And soon they were getting together every weekend, sometimes multiple nights in a row. And she never held out for that kiss or worried about her hair or her clothes or other things that might have made her nervous with a new guy she was spending time with. It wasn't something she could have done with someone else, not if they were dating, not if there had been interest. With Ethan, it had been about more than interest. It had been about connection.

She stared at the bubbles in her champagne, watching them float around. Her cheek still tingled from where he'd kissed her.

"Aw, now, you can do better than that!" Milly jeered, giving Ethan a look of naked disapproval. "Give the girl a real kiss."

Claire stiffened in panic. She tried to think of a polite excuse, maybe that she didn't really like public displays of affection, but that seemed lame and almost rude. They were at a rehearsal dinner for a wedding, after all, and this was hardly a public venue. It was a family party, celebrating life and love.

She looked up at Ethan, hoping he could sense the angst in her eyes, the flash of warning they liked to use on each other when it was time to exit a party or, like last night, disentangle themselves from uncomfortable conversation. But Ethan just gave her a slow grin and wrapped his other arm around her waist until she was properly facing him. Her heart was thumping out of her chest now, so loudly she was sure everyone in the room could hear it, even above the music, but Ethan didn't waver. His smile slipped as he dipped his head, and oh boy, it was happening. He was kissing her. Her best friend, confidant, keeper of secrets and righter of wrongs was now creeping closer and closer to her face until—

She closed her eyes just before his lips met hers. His mouth was soft but firm, and she parted her lips ever so slightly, as he kissed her once, letting it linger. It was simple. But oh, it was way more than boring.

Claire pulled back, flitted her eyes to the pleased smiles of Ethan's relatives, and took a hearty sip of her drink, not daring to look in Ethan's direction.

Maybe it was for show. Maybe it was part of the act.

But it felt real.

And more than that, it felt right.

Chapter Nine

Claire brushed her fingers over her lips and stared at the ceiling, listening to Ethan's steady breath on the other side of the extra tall pile of rolled towels. She turned her head, barely daring to exhale for fear of waking him, and her pulse skipped when she watched him roll over, flinging an arm straight across her, undeterred by the barrier she'd so carefully built last night.

She looked away. Straight at the ceiling and its big, exposed beams, the very ones that Ethan had played on as a child. His arm was heavy on her stomach, and she wondered for a fleeting second if he was awake, doing this on purpose, to rile her up, or . . .

She held her breath, listened to his . . . No. He was asleep. Besides, why would he be doing this on purpose? So they'd kissed. Really, what was the big deal? They were two adults, two individuals who were playing a part. Had she thought they wouldn't kiss at all during this charade?

Actually, she hadn't thought about it at all. And now it was all she could do not to think about it. That and the warm sensation of his hand on her stomach. She tipped her chin awkwardly, wondering if she could subtly shift her body until she was free, but that would only wake him, and she wasn't so sure she was ready for that.

All night long, every time she drifted off, she relived that kiss: the way his eyes had dropped as his face had neared, the way her heart had sped up with anticipation, and that first jolt when his mouth hit hers, softly, gently, expertly. Part of her had wanted to push him off. She'd always assumed that kissing Ethan would be like kissing a brother. Sure, he was cute, but she didn't see him in that way. Except now maybe she did. And that kiss was far from platonic. No, it was slow and tender and . . .

Crazy! The man was her best friend. Her best friend who had asked her to pose as his girlfriend. Her best friend who didn't date, not seriously. He'd probably kissed at least two other girls within the past week. Last night surely meant nothing to him.

Clearly he wasn't losing any sleep over it, she thought, slanting his sleeping body a hard glance as she began to feel irritated.

She slid out from under the weight of his arm, balancing one foot on the floor until she was able to completely slide out, nearly stumbling onto the floor. She eyed Ethan watchfully. He appeared to still be sleeping.

Good. She grabbed a heap of clothes from her suitcase and padded into the bathroom to change. She'd take a walk on the beach, maybe even venture into town. And when she returned . . . Well, that kiss would be forgotten.

*

Ethan stood in his mother's kitchen, sipping coffee and listening to the birds sing through the open windows. His sisters were nowhere to be seen—they'd apparently gone into town early to get their hair and nails attended to well before this afternoon's festivities.

He relished in their absence, even though Leslie seemed to have forgiven last summer's mishap; fortunately the friend was now in a serious relationship and very happy.

He frowned a little at that thought. Everyone was pairing up, settling down, finding someone they connected with and trusted. Except Claire, he thought. Claire was free. For now. And loath as he was to admit it, he didn't like the thought of her falling for another Matt. He'd barely tolerated every interaction he had with the guy, even though he was easy enough to talk to and didn't have any bad qualities, per se, other than breaking Claire's heart, of course. That was unforgiveable. But the next guy might stick around a little longer, and why shouldn't he? Claire was a catch. Any guy could see that.

He set the mug down on the counter heavily. Wasn't he a lousy friend? He should want Claire to be happy.

And he did. Just not with someone else.

And that was just plain unfair of him.

"Claire is quite a hit around here," his mother confessed. She was sitting at the kitchen table near the big bay window, carefully measuring polished pebbles into the bottom of what she'd told him was a hurricane jar, to be used for the candles that would decorate tonight's reception. "I must say she's lived up to everything you said about her, and you certainly weren't shy with the praise."

No, he hadn't been, and everything he'd said was the truth. He rubbed his chin, feeling a day's worth of stubble prickle his fingers, and wondered what that said about him. "Claire is a wonderful woman," he replied.

His mother stopped scooping the stones and stared at him, a smile breaking her face as she clasped her hands to her chest.

Ethan shook his head in warning. "Now don't go getting ahead of yourself, Mom. I just said she's wonderful. I didn't say I was going to marry her." For a moment he dared to imagine what it might be like to be married to Claire. They'd argue over where to live, and God knew their ideas of tasteful decorating varied—he preferred sleek and modern while she preferred something cozier and, admittedly, homier. But for the most part, it wouldn't be much different than it was now. They'd go out to dinner, or order a pizza and watch television; they'd share the details of their days, listening with genuine interest, knowing their histories so well.

They'd find something funny even in the worst parts of their stories; they had a knack for that. And the next morning, it would start again. Another day with Claire. More time with Claire.

He was always up for more time with Claire, he thought. But could the same be said for her?

"Claire and I are just—" He'd been about to say friends. "We're taking it slow."

He frowned at this. Maybe they were taking it slow. Maybe this was all leading to something. Or maybe on a June Saturday like this one, he'd be sipping coffee, waiting to go to Claire's wedding, to watch her promise herself to another man. To know that someone else would forever enjoy her laughter, her wit, her loyalty, while he ...

He rubbed a hand over his jaw. Better not to think about that.

His mother went back to measuring the stones. "I just want you to be happy."

"I am happy, Mom," he assured her, and he realized that he wasn't just saying that to protect her. It was the first time that he'd been back to Grey Harbor when he felt relaxed, at peace, even whole. He was happy, but then, he was always happy with Claire.

His phone beeped and he checked the screen. Claire had sent him a message before he'd woken up to let him know she was getting an early start in town, and that she wanted to spend a bit more time in some of Grey Harbor's many antique shops. He was always game for a shopping trip, but his patience faded after ten or fifteen minutes, whereas Claire could spend hours poking around dusty shops, delightfully pointing out details about things that really didn't interest him very much, not that he ever let on. He always knew when something was special, because her eyes would start to dance and conversation would stop, and a little circle of wonder would form on her pretty lips. Sometimes it was something odd, like a small silver spoon or a dusty oil painting, not that he was focused much on the objects. No, he was always focused on Claire. Her face. Her mannerisms. Her smile.

Right. "I should probably head out and meet Claire." He leaned over and gave his mother a kiss on the cheek.

"Have fun," she said, returning to her centerpiece arrangements.

Ethan grabbed an apple from the fruit bowl in the center of the breakfast bar, but hesitated at the screen door. "You sure you don't want me to stick around and help? I don't mind."

"With this project?" His mother raised an eyebrow and Ethan barked out a laugh. "You go have fun, Claire is waiting for you. Besides, believe it or not, sometimes I like it when the house is empty. It gives me time to reminisce."

"Reminisce?" Ethan wasn't so sure he liked the sound of that.

She gave a wistful smile. "Oh, about the old days. When you were all little. When your father was still here. We had so many wonderful conversations at this very table." Her brow pinched a little as she looked out the window onto the water. "He's still with me, though. So long as I'm in this house. So long as I'm in Grey Harbor. Every corner holds a memory."

Ethan jutted his lip, feeling a familiar wave of guilt hit him square in the gut. "I'm sorry I haven't visited more often, Mom."

She brushed his concern away as she reached for another candle. "You're young. Busy. I understand. You have your exciting life in the city."

"It's not that exciting." If anything it was tiring. Sometimes he didn't know why he bothered anymore—going out under the guise of research for his articles was old habit. A habit he was afraid to break, if he was honest with himself.

"Maybe now that you and Claire have been up here together, you'll come again. I think she'd like that." His mother's gaze turned hopeful.

"I think she would," Ethan thought aloud. And he would, too.

*

Claire was sitting on a bench outside Grey Harbor's bakery, eating what appeared to be a giant cinnamon roll. This wasn't like her. She only ate like that when she was one of two things: very stressed or very happy. He slowed his pace, wondering which it was. Up until this weekend he would have said she was very stressed. But here in

Grey Harbor, he'd seen a hint of the old Claire returning. The carefree, fun-loving Claire he couldn't get enough of.

Ethan frowned with curiosity as she indulged in another bite, swinging one long leg that was crossed casually over the other, her flip-flop dangling from her toes. Up until now he hadn't thought of that kiss—told himself it was part of the act, that he'd been encouraged by Aunt Milly, that he hadn't chosen to do it all.

Except now . . . Now he couldn't help thinking he'd like to do it again. And soon.

She turned suddenly, flashing him a smile when she spotted him, and held up the pastry. "Want a bite?"

Ethan thrust his hands into his pockets and walked the rest of the way to the bench. "Nah, I'm good. My mom fed me a big breakfast this morning."

"That sounds promising," she said, polishing off the last piece of the roll. She licked the last of the icing from her thumb, and Ethan watched her mouth, his stomach tightening as her lips pursed, and then looked away, down onto the street, where weekend tourists were already out shopping. Kimberly could be amongst them, he supposed. He shifted uneasily on the bench.

"It was a nice morning," he confided, still not looking directly at Claire. "I'm enjoying myself here more this time."

"Why do you think that is?" Claire asked, and he turned to look her in the eye.

Because of you, he thought, but then shrugged instead. "Who knows. Everyone is getting along better. Maybe it's because they're not on my case about my wild ways." He frowned at that. Last year he'd been on the outs with every member of the family; his aunts had looked at him with scorn, his mother with disappointment. And his sisters . . .

He grew quiet, watched a bird peck at the crumbs on the ground.

He didn't like the person he'd become. The person his family saw him as. And this time around . . . Well, everything just felt right.

Claire stood up and deposited her paper bag into a nearby trash bin. "So, how should we spend our last day in Grey Harbor?"

Ethan hadn't given it much thought, but now he knew exactly where he wanted to go. Somewhere he hadn't been in too long. Somewhere he'd avoided. Like so much else in his life. The fishing dock was just at the border of town, on the northern edge of the harbor. They didn't talk much as they walked, just took in the sights and sounds, the fresh air.

"Hailey called again," Claire said, breaking the silence.

He raised an eyebrow. "Let me guess. You still haven't called back."

Claire shook her head. "I think this is a conversation that needs to happen in person, as tough as it will be. I just wish I could figure out what to do next. I can't take shifts at the café forever."

"I've always thought you should do something

different with your background. Take a risk. When's the last time you did that?"

He hesitated. He wasn't sure when the last time was that he'd taken a risk. It was easier somehow to choose the safe route, even if it left him bored and unfulfilled and sometimes even a little depressed.

"Yes, but what? My background is at an auction house. I've applied to all the museums. It's probably time to start over."

"What about opening your own shop?" he suggested.

"An antique shop?" She looked at him quizzically. "I love perusing them, but operating one . . ." She shook her head. "I don't see how I could stand out."

"What about vintage clothes? Or vintage jewelry? You have an eye for that type of thing. And I think a project would do you good."

She smiled at him. "I like that. I like that a lot." She licked her bottom lip as she mulled the idea, her lashes fluttering as she blinked. "Why didn't I ever think of it myself?"

"Because you've been too clouded thinking about other things," he pointed out. "I know what's best for you, Claire."

They locked eyes for a beat and Ethan glanced away. Thrusting his hands into his pockets, he kept walking, hoping the sand beneath his feet would pound out the emotions that were building, the idea that was planted, that he couldn't shake.

He'd kissed her, damn it. Tasted her. He'd always

imagined what it might be like, the single mystery that he was yet to experience, and now he had. And it had been better than he could have imagined. Sweet and familiar and so damn sexy. He could still hear the gasp of her breath just before his lips found hers, felt her hesitation before she relaxed into the moment.

Ethan stayed quiet as the boats came into sight as well as the little shack where he and his dad would buy worms to tackle. There were many spots they could have settled, but he was here, and now that he was, it didn't seem right to sit anywhere other than the spot near the rocks, where he and his dad would spend many quiet weekend mornings, waiting for a fish to bite.

"Looking forward to the wedding tonight?" Claire asked as she smoothed her blue cotton skirt over her thighs.

Ethan shifted his gaze, swallowing hard. "I just hope Amelia holds herself together tonight." She'd cried through most of Leslie's wedding last year, but given her recent broken heart, that had been forgiven. Ethan's behavior, on the other hand . . .

"It can't be easy for her," Claire said. "Weddings are a tough reminder for the broken-hearted."

"Not a source of hope?" he cajoled, even though he knew what she meant. And he understood. More than she knew.

"Oh, weddings, you know . . . I keep thinking of how I used to dream about my own wedding. Now the man I thought might be my husband is marrying someone else!" She laughed, but her emotions betrayed her and it came out more like a strangled sob.

He looked her square in the eye. "You know what I say? I say forget him. He's not worth your time. He's not worth your tears."

"I know," Claire said, nodding furiously. She wiped at her cheeks. "I know, but . . ."

"Can I tell you something, Claire? That guy was never right for you. Yeah, he was nice enough, and sort of fun to hang out with, but he didn't care about you the way that he should have." There. He'd said it. He'd been holding it in, keeping it bottled up for fear of ticking her off—or losing her. But he couldn't sit here and watch her cry over someone so undeserving any longer.

"Why do you say that?" Claire asked.

"He broke your heart, Claire. What more needs to be said?" Only more did need to be said. There was no excuse for Matt to not send flowers, much less a card, when Claire's mother had died, or to have gone along with pretending it had never happened. Ethan had seen the pain in her eyes firsthand, been there with her family, felt her anguish, felt it deep down, just like it had been when his own parent was lost.

"He might have ended things, but that didn't mean he never deserved me. It doesn't mean what we had wasn't real." She was standing up, fumbling with her skirt, marching off down the dock, her sandals clutched in her fist.

"Claire!" he called after her, but it was useless. She was gone, running off along the path to the beach, the sand kicking up against her heels. He watched until she slowed her pace to a fast, determined walk, and then resumed her jog, with a little less energy.

He could catch her if he wanted to, run after her, grab her, and tell her he was sorry. But he wasn't completely sorry. The truth was that he'd meant what he'd said. He wanted her to be over this man, done with it, finished. And not just because the guy had never deserved her, even if she'd excused his less than admirable behavior time and time again.

The truth was that he didn't like Claire having feelings for someone else. Not when he was starting to realize that the only person he wanted her to have any feeling for was him.

*

Claire furiously brushed at a hot tear that dripped down her cheek and dropped onto the sand next to a lifeguard stand. She winced as she set a hand to her side; the stitch was fierce, and she was panting, sweating, too. She'd never been much of a runner. She'd barely made it two laps around the goalposts back in middle school, and poor Hailey, who could easily jog a mile without much effort, would hop along beside her, offering encouragement until Claire breathlessly urged her to go ahead, and then watched as her cousin's ponytail bounced along her back.

Ethan knew that Claire couldn't run. It was a joke of theirs. And she knew he could run. He'd finished two Chicago marathons, and he didn't even wear them like a badge of honor or anything. It was just something he'd done for the heck of it, not to boast about. But then, Ethan didn't boast.

She supposed it was one of his good qualities. Right up with telling the truth. Even when you didn't want to hear it, even when he was breaking a heart, or letting someone down, or even inviting them home, she knew that he always told it straight, didn't mislead, didn't lie.

Well, he'd certainly told it to her straight just now, hadn't he?

She pressed her fingers deeper into her side, wincing. The pain in her abdomen would go away soon, she knew, but the ache in her chest . . . Ethan had hit a nerve.

She followed the shore to where the clouds billowed in the deep blue sky. *Oh, crap.* He was coming.

She looked around for a place to run and hide, to get away, but the beach was bare aside from a young family building a sandcastle, and besides, there was no way around it. She was in Grey Harbor. And Ethan was her ride home.

And she didn't like being mad at Ethan, truth be told. It rarely happened. It made her feel strangely, horribly alone.

"I'm sorry," he said as he approached. "I should have chosen my words more carefully. I didn't mean to be insensitive."

"But you meant what you said?"

His gaze was steady. "I always do."

Her shoulders deflated a bit. "I know. And you were right, too. But the truth hurts sometimes."

"Am I allowed to sit here?" He didn't wait for an answer before dropping onto the sand next to her. "You know what I meant, Claire. You have too much life ahead of you to spend thinking about a man that didn't deserve you. It didn't mean it wasn't right to care about him. But learn from it, and move on. You'll be happier in the end. I know it."

"You really believe that?" she asked, her voice cracking a bit.

He nodded, giving her a slow smile. His eyes were sincere. "I do."

She looked out onto the water, finding hope in his conviction.

"You know that girl I mentioned . . . Kimberly. When I told you I thought about marrying her, I wasn't entirely forthcoming." Ethan paused. "We were engaged."

Claire blinked in disbelief. She tried to wrap her head around it, but she couldn't. The Ethan she knew was lighthearted and laid-back, with no thoughts to the future, no holds on the past. He'd never expressed emotional interest in a single woman he'd casually dated over the years. Certainly never discussed the desire to be married.

"So you called it off?" It made sense, she supposed,

given his track record. She shook her head. Poor girl.

"Not exactly," he said, giving a wry grin. "She did."

She did? But that meant . . . "So all that talk about not wanting to settle down, wanting to enjoy your youth?"

He shrugged. "We do what we can to get through. We tell ourselves what we need to believe."

She stared at him in wonder. All this time she'd thought that Ethan wasn't capable of falling in love. But the truth was he was no different than her. Broken-hearted. Maybe a little lost.

"We're quite a pair," she chuckled. She looked up at him, watching his profile as he stared out onto the stretch of sand. She followed his gaze to the young family, watching as a boy of about three carried a bucket of water back from the lake. It sloshed and tipped and splashed against his feet, his parents laughed and told him to try again.

Because that's what you did, she supposed. You tried again.

"Are you still . . . in love with her?" It felt weird to ask that, to talk about Ethan's love life. So often they talked about hers, Ethan playing the cynic. She supposed that was what he had become.

"It was years ago," he said. "But I'm no masochist."

"So you don't think you'll ever find love again?" She felt sad at the thought of it, wondering if Ethan felt empty by his casual dating, or if instead he found it liberating.

He met her gaze, his expression earnest and

unreadable and possibly even a little suggestive. Claire thought back to that kiss, to how natural it felt, how warm and exciting and tingling all at once.

More like an exercise in practice, she thought. She stopped herself. *Now who sounded cynical?*

"I want to believe I can find love again," he surprised her by saying. "I want you to believe that, too."

Chapter Ten

Claire hugged her arms around her waist and watched as the bride and groom made their way onto the dance floor, Meryl beaming as she held hands with her husband and he twirled her in front of the band, making the satin skirt of her dress swoosh.

The sun had faded over an hour ago, leaving the room dark and romantic, lit by strings of fairy lights wrapped in potted trees and candles flickering in their glass containers. Through the French doors that lined the east wall, Lake Michigan shimmered in the moonlight.

Even Amelia seemed to have a little smile on her face, Claire noted from across the room. Ethan's younger sister seemed softer tonight; the little pinch between her eyebrows was gone. She was really quite pretty, Claire realized, but then she wasn't so sure why she was surprised. Ethan's family was beautiful—inside and out. Eddie, the groom, was a lucky man to be marrying into it.

"Penny for your thoughts," Ethan said, coming to stand beside her.

Claire felt her cheeks flush. In his dark suit and summery lavender tie he looked particularly handsome tonight. Not that every other eligible girl in the room hadn't noticed, she thought, eyeing a passing waitress who slipped an appreciative smile his way.

"Oh, I was just thinking how pretty this reception is. The candles. The flowers."

Ethan nodded. "Almost enough to make you want to plan your own wedding, isn't it?"

Startled, Claire looked up at him, but he was staring out onto the lake. Marriage seemed to be something he disdained, or at least, hoped to delay. But maybe that was all bravado talking, the voice of a broken heart, trying to convince himself that he didn't want the one thing he couldn't have.

They stood in silence, watching as the bride and groom finished their first dance, and slowly other couples joined them in the center of the room as the music subtly shifted to the next song. If it was a faster beat, no doubt Ethan would have run out to join them—he loved a good party—but with the soft, slow tune, she supposed she may as well sample the dessert buffet. Someone had mentioned chocolate-covered strawberries, and those might go nicely with one last glass of champagne.

She was just about to suggest it to Ethan when she realized he was staring at her, his eyebrow cocked in invitation; her lips curved into a mischievous grin.

"What?" she asked, warily eyeing him.

He tipped his head ever so slightly to the dance floor, his expression unwavering, and Claire felt her stomach flip over. He was asking her to dance with him. Not a fast dance. A slow dance.

They didn't need to, she knew. No one was watching them. For once, tonight, all attention was on the bride and groom, as it should be. Claire hesitated, waiting for her pulse to resume a normal speed, and then, because Ethan was impossible to resist, especially when he had his mind set on something, nodded. To turn him down seemed wrong, and she realized she didn't want to. She wanted to feel his arms around her, enjoy this night, with its soft lighting and its promise of romance, and feel like she belonged to someone. Belonged to Ethan, maybe.

They stepped out onto the dance floor, and before she had even prepared herself, he set a firm arm around her waist, pulling her close as his other hand met hers. She swallowed hard, feeling the beat of his heart against her chest, looking over his shoulder at the other guests, chatting and swaying across the candlelit room.

"Remember those tango lessons we took that one time?" Ethan's grin was wicked when she craned her neck to look up at him.

Claire laughed. She'd nearly forgotten. He'd won it in some raffle at work, all but begged her to come with him, and she had . . . only to discover that the partners were "random" so Ethan got to dance with the beautiful, and most likely single, instructor, while Claire toddled along with an eighty-year-old retired professor who couldn't have been much more than five feet tall and kept letting his hand slip to her backside.

Without any warning, Ethan tightened his grip on her hand and led them sternly across the floor, weaving where needed between couples in an effortless way. Claire let out a whoop of delight as he reached the end of the dance floor and abruptly turned her, steering her in the opposite direction. The moves slowly came back to her, still a little muddled, and she did the best she could, amazed at how much he remembered. As the song came to end, Ethan expertly spun her around and then, to her complete astonishment, flung her dramatically into a dip.

She tossed her head back, laughing as he carefully brought her up. "You've been practicing," she said, poking him in the chest.

He gave a bashful grin. "Maybe once or twice. It's come in handy at times."

Her heart sank a little. He was who he was, a man with well-practiced maneuvers and easy charm. She should know better than to be falling for them.

"I was always a little disappointed I got stuck with that dance instructor that night," he confessed, and Claire frowned. She blinked at the ground, officially sobered. When she looked up at him, his eyes were twinkling with amusement. "But it was worth it to see you getting groped by that dirty old man."

"He wasn't a dirty old man!" Claire protested, but she was laughing again. "His hand kept slipping. He was frail. Okay, he was a dirty old man." She gave him a smile, but he didn't return it. His eyes had shifted, somewhere in the distance, just over her shoulder. She turned, wondering what was there, but all she saw was a crowd of guests coming and going through the main doors to the hall.

"What do you say we get out of here?" he whispered, glancing at her for approval.

She held her breath, knowing what he meant in those few simple words. It was something he'd said before. It rolled of his tongue with ease. But it was the first time he'd suggested it to her. Of course, any other night she wouldn't have read into it this way. She would have assumed he was ready to leave, get on with the night, not take her home. But something had shifted between them, there was something crackling under the surface, a new tension that needed release.

"I'd like that," she said, feeling her heart skip a beat, and this time, she didn't even stiffen when he reached down and took her hand and led her away from the crowd.

*

Ethan didn't want to go back to the boathouse. It felt too stifling, too small, and too tempting, for that matter. If they went back to that little room, he wasn't sure what would happen, and he needed to make sure anything that happened tonight was right. For both of them.

The hammock was swaying in the breeze when they climbed out of the car and took the stone path into the backyard. Ethan walked over to it and hopped on, holding out a hand to Claire. She grinned at him, even in the light from the moon he could see her face clearly, and took his hand. The hammock swayed under their weight, causing Claire to giggle as they settled their bodies, finally lying side by side to gaze up at the stars.

"I don't think I've seen a sky like this in years," Claire marveled. She was whispering, even though there was no one around, but in the still night, he heard her clearly.

He pointed up at one of his favorite constellations. "You don't see the stars in the city. Not this clearly, anyhow."

"Looking forward to getting back?" she asked.

"Not really," he admitted. "You?"

"Not really," she replied, and then shivered.

Ethan wriggled out of his suit coat, causing the hammock to sway precariously to the ground—he had to set his foot down to steady them. Finally, he pulled the jacket free and draped it over Claire's torso. "Better?" he asked, settling back against the pillow again.

"You're too good to me," she said, pulling the coat up around her chin.

"I could say the same back to you," he said. He stared up at the vast sky, relaxing into the moment. "I have to thank you, Claire. For going along with this . . . ruse. I haven't enjoyed my time here in a while. It's because of you."

He heard a soft rustling beside him. Claire never had been good at accepting compliments. "Happy to help," she finally said.

He knew he could have let it go there, but he felt compelled to push, to explain, to somehow make clear this restlessness he felt. This urge to press their cozy situation. To see how great things could be.

"I know we've been playing a part, but you've made me see Grey Harbor a little differently. The way I used to see it. The good parts."

"There are a lot of things to love here," she agreed.

He turned to look at her, surprised to meet her eyes. His pulse kicked as his gaze roamed her face, trailing from her lashes to her lips. He swallowed hard, hearing the beat of his heart cut through the silence. "There are."

He leaned in, almost not daring to take this step but not willing to let the moment go, either. This was deliberate, chosen, there was no Aunt Milly egging him on. He didn't know how Claire would react, but he wouldn't know unless he tried. And he had to try, damn it. He couldn't fight it anymore.

Her lips were soft and warm, and she opened her mouth to him, letting him kiss her deeply, slowly, as his arm came around her waist, pulling her to him. He pushed the suit coat away, grazing his fingers over the thin, silky material of her dress, pressing his chest against hers until he felt the swell of her breasts, the beat of her heart.

He kissed her mouth, her neck, her cheeks, feeling their connection transition from friendship to lover, as easily as if it had been headed that way all along, whether or not either of them had been ready to admit it.

Chapter Eleven

Even before Claire opened her eyes, she knew that something was different. No, that something had changed. There had been a shift, a risk that she'd taken. She stirred, stiffening as she felt a weight holding her in place.

Ethan was behind her, his arm wrapped firmly around her waist. He was rousing, she could feel it. She braced herself, made up an excuse, and steeled herself for the inevitable. Convinced herself that it didn't matter what had happened last night, that they could go back to being friends, that nothing had to change. But something had changed.

The hammock swayed as Ethan moved, and Claire darted her eyes to the house, wondering if they'd been spotted by his mother and sisters. She pulled the suit coat a little higher, even though she was still wearing her dress. They'd made love slowly last night, tenderly, never fully disrobing even, careful not to rock the hammock, or perhaps just careful to enjoy the moment. She couldn't be sure anymore. It felt like a dream, a blurry, vague experience that might not have even happened. Except it had. And lying here, with the sun beating down through the willow branches and the birds chirping ahead was her proof.

Ethan opened one eye and then the other. His mouth tipped into a slow grin that made her heart roll over. "Good morning," he said, his voice gravelly and deep.

"Hey," she said, smiling back, laughing when he pulled her a little closer, nuzzling into the crook of her neck.

He kissed her again, nibbling her neck, making her squirm with pleasure, but when she opened her eyes, she pulled back hard, nearly falling off the hammock until Ethan was quick to reach out an arm and catch her.

"Jesus!" he cried. "That eager to get away from me, are you?"

She shot him a look of warning. "Your mother," she hissed, motioning toward the house with her chin.

Barbara was standing at the base of the patio, staring at them with wide eyes, one hip turned as if she was trying to flee but hadn't been quick enough. When Ethan turned to see what was going on, Barbara rearranged her expression into a smile and waved cheerfully. "I was just coming down to see if you're coming to the wedding brunch," she called. "But I can see you're already up."

"What time is it?" Claire asked, puzzled.

Ethan checked his watch. "Nine. We slept in."

"That's the best sleep I've had in months," Claire marveled, relieved to see Barbara retreating into the house. She looked at Ethan, wondering if she should say something, ask what had happened last night, if they knew what they were doing, or if they had simply gotten caught up in the parts they were playing.

But then she felt his hand come up and brush a strand of hair from her cheek. Ethan grinned at her before leaning in for a quick kiss. "Me too."

*

The wedding brunch was held at Milly's house, another lakeside property a bit farther up the beach. While a bit smaller than her sister Barbara's home, Milly's white Cape was bursting with lilac bushes and charm. Quirky stone ducks guided their walk up to the big back porch, where a long table was set up for the meal. Vases of fresh lilacs were scattered over the surface, which was covered in a crisp white tablecloth. Servers were passing champagne cocktails and a chef's station was set up near the edge of the deck, near a coffee stand.

"This is so elaborate," Claire mused, taking it all in. She almost said she now hoped to have something like it when she got married, but she managed to stop herself just in time. She couldn't exactly say things like that to Ethan now, could she? Not after last night.

Eventually, they'd have to talk, but for now . . . She looked down to where his hand held hers, then up and around the beautiful white sprawling deck with views of the still waters of Lake Michigan. For now she would just enjoy the moment. Before long they'd be in the car, heading back to the city.

Back to reality, she thought, all at once filled with dread. Back to sleeping on Hailey's couch and searching for a job. And back to just being Ethan's best friend?

She felt him watching her and flashed him an involuntary grin, even though her stomach felt a little uneasy and her heart was fluttering in a way it probably shouldn't. They were on vacation, swept up in one beautiful and romantic party after the next, without a care in the world. As much as she wished she could keep this going forever, she knew she couldn't.

Still, as Ethan dropped her hand, he just as quickly set it on the small of her back, his eyes taking on a gleam as they walked to the buffet. Claire had to laugh. Some things were still the same, and that was reassuring.

They filled their plates and took a seat at the far end of the table, near some of Ethan's cousins, a rowdy bunch that were roughly her age. Ethan introduced her to the men, who she was told now lived all over the country, from Seattle to Boston.

"This is almost like a family reunion then," she commented, thinking of what a nice weekend it must be for them all. Hailey was her only cousin, and while they were as close as sisters, she had always longed for the bustle of a big, dynamic family like this one.

The cousin with mischievous clear blue eyes grinned at Ethan. "Ethan here had a reunion all of his own last night. Isn't that right, Eth?"

Claire frowned. "What do you mean?"

But the guy was looking past her, straight at Ethan, whose jaw had gone tense as he set down his fork. "Ethan knows what I mean. Kimberly's hard to miss."

"Kimberly was there last night?" Claire's voice croaked as the realization hit hard. "Did you see her?" But of course he had. Silly girl. It was all becoming clear now.

Ethan's eyes darkened with admittance, and she didn't need to wait for him to speak to know the answer. She managed to choke down the last of her coffee, and then stood on shaky legs. "Think I'll get a refill."

Only she didn't go to the coffee stand. Instead, she handed her mug to the nearest member of the catering staff and casually walked down the stairs to the lawn, even though her heart was pounding and all she wanted to do was break into a mad sprint.

Ethan was behind her, she could hear his feet on the steps as she hit the grass, but she didn't stop. She walked as quickly as she could without making a scene, not turning around until she was hidden by a row of evergreens, out of sight.

"So that's what last night was all about that?" She folded her arms across her chest; the blood was rushing in her ears. "You saw Kimberly. Your ex-fiancée."

Ethan dragged a hand through his hair. "It wasn't like that. It doesn't matter."

"I'm not going to be your rebound girl," she said, pushing past him. She'd already been there, done that once, and look where it had gotten her.

"You weren't my rebound girl," he said, grabbing her by the elbow.

"Then what am I?" She locked his eyes while she waited for his answer. For a moment she wavered. This was Ethan, for crying out loud! Her best friend, the man who knew her best. He was her person. Someone she couldn't live without. And here she was, pushing him away.

Or maybe he'd pushed her away.

She blinked back the tears that prickled the back of her eyes. She couldn't cry. Not now. When she was sad or hurting, Ethan was the one she ran to. But if he was the one making her cry, then who was there?

Hailey, she thought, suddenly longing to be back in Chicago, in that cramped Lincoln Park apartment, a pizza on the coffee table and a box of tissues at her side. What would Hailey have to say about this?

Fool, that's what she'd say, or at least what she'd imply. And she'd be right. A man like Ethan . . . What had she been thinking?

"What are you, Claire?" Ethan repeated. "You know how much you mean to me."

Claire's shoulders began to ache from tension. She

realized she was shaking. She nodded, but she didn't even know what she was agreeing to anymore. She did know how much she meant to Ethan. She knew she was his closest friend. But was she more?

"I don't want to lose you. I can't lose you." His jaw pulsed and Claire felt a wave of panic wash over her. "It's me, Claire. I know it's the oldest cliché out there, but it's not you. It's me. You're the best friend I've ever had. I don't want to lose that."

"Who said you'd lose it?" she asked, blinking fast.

"I messed up. I should have left things alone. I got caught up in this fake relationship."

Of course. She should have known. "You got caught up." She shook her head in disgust and turned to leave, but he grabbed her hand, pulling her back to him. She snatched it away, her eyes blazing. She didn't want to hear anymore. He'd said all there was. He'd gotten caught up, and she was there, a convenient side dish to the weekend.

"I didn't mean it that way. I meant, being with you, here, in Grey Harbor, pretending you were my girlfriend, holding your hand, even kissing you . . . it was nice, Claire. It made me feel things."

She swallowed the lump in her throat. "It made me feel things too."

"But look at us now. Look at what's happening!" There was a pain in his eyes she didn't think she'd ever seen before, and it startled her. "We never fight. We never hurt each other. One night together and everything is already unraveling."

She couldn't argue with him there. Sadness filled her when she thought of everything they'd lost. Years of friendship and laughter, hours of conversation . . . She didn't see how it could ever be that way again. Every time she tried, she saw his mouth, that quirk of his smile, that look in his eyes right before he'd kissed her.

"I can't lose you, Claire." His eyes were pleading, but she didn't care. Couldn't care. Couldn't give in. She couldn't go back to being his friend, the girl at the bar who listened while he played back his latest dates, or sit back and watch him break another heart.

Because this time, he'd broken hers.

"Too late," she said, and turned and ran before he could see her cry.

*

Claire had already put a call into a cab company by the time she got back to the cottage; chances were, the driver would know his way to the nearest bus terminal, and with any luck, she'd be able to slip away before anyone was back from the brunch.

She changed into something more casual for travel and quickly stuffed her suitcase, cursing under her breath at how much she'd brought as she wrestled with the zipper. Finally, she got it closed and did her best to awkwardly drag it out of the cottage, forcing herself to not look back, to not dwell on her time here, or how nice it had all seemed.

The main house was empty, but Claire felt a tug in her chest as she passed by it on her way to the driveway, wishing she could have had a chance to give Barbara a proper good-bye, even though there was no sense in holding on, or forging more of a connection. She'd probably never see any of these people again. The thought saddened her.

She was just coming around the stone path when she saw Amelia skip out the side door. Claire stilled as her mind began to race, wondering how she would explain this one, but Amelia just slid on her sunglasses and pressed a code to open the garage door.

"Looks like you're headed out," she remarked, as the carriage doors slid open. She gave Claire the once-over. "Ethan isn't with you?"

"Oh, I . . ." Claire managed a shaky grin. "I need to get back early." It was true. Very true. She needed to get back. To Chicago. To her life. To Hailey. To put distance between herself and this place and everything that had happened here.

Amelia jingled her keys. "Help me with my bags and I'll give you a ride."

"You're going to Chicago?" Claire stared at Ethan's sister in wonder.

"Time for a change," Amelia said, grinning.

Claire felt her own smile relax as she helped Amelia load her bags into the car. Amelia made several trips into the house, the screen door banging loudly in her wake each time. Eventually they crammed it all in, somehow managing to fit Claire's bag in the backseat.

"So . . ." Amelia said, as Claire slipped into the front passenger seat. The air in the car felt thick and stale and she cranked the window, eager for one last taste of the morning breeze. "You and Ethan have a fight?"

Claire shrugged. "Oh . . ."

"You can be straight with me, you know. I get it. I know that look. It's in your eyes." She clucked her tongue in disappointment as she put the car in reverse and began the slow pull from the driveway.

Claire watched sadly as the house grew smaller. A part of her wanted to get out, run, to talk to Ethan and make things right, but she didn't know how anymore. Too much had changed.

"Ethan has a way of disappointing women," Amelia said as they drove down the road into town. "But I thought you might be different. He was different with you." She looked at her sharply. "You guys are friends. Good friends. Am I right?"

"How'd you know?" Claire asked in surprise.

Amelia raised an eyebrow. "For starters, you know him too well. Other women just see the good looks and outgoing personality. You saw through him. And, you practically blanched every time he touched you." She paused. "But then you'd get this little smile on your face, like it was something new, something special. You like him, don't you? As more than friends?"

No, she told herself firmly. The answer should be no,

that Ethan was her friend, that they could move past this, that she didn't imagine him as anything more, didn't want to be anything more than he already was.

But she just couldn't say that.

Claire stared out the window at the trees whirring by. "It doesn't matter."

"Damn straight it matters!" Amelia slammed a palm on the steering wheel and Claire jumped. "It matters, Claire," Amelia said again, her passion growing with the pink in her cheeks. "Life is short. I learned that when my father died. And love . . . well, if there isn't love, then what is there? What's the point?"

Claire gave a small smile. She and Amelia had more in common than Ethan probably wished to be true. "Sometimes being friends can be fulfilling enough." And it had been. For nearly four years, it had been enough.

Ethan was right. They'd gone and messed up. Ruined it.

She stared back out the window miserably.

Amelia was quiet for a minute. Finally she flicked off the radio and said, "Did Ethan ever tell you the details of my broken heart?"

Claire slowly faced her, afraid to admit just how curious she was. "He just said that there was someone who you were struggling to get over."

Amelia snorted. "You could say that again. I gave it my all. It didn't work out. Some people might think I'm silly. Or even pathetic. They've tolerated me. But I had to see it through. I had to wait, see if he'd change his mind. He didn't. And . . . he won't. And I can sit around crying about it for another year, or can I pick myself up and find my own happy ending. Last night was inspiring, wasn't it?"

Claire felt the urge to reach over and give the poor girl a hug. "It hurts, doesn't it?"

Amelia shrugged, her eyes fixed on the road. "At least I know I tried. I held out hope. Nothing wrong with that, really. Not if you really loved someone."

"You know, last week I sold my ex-boyfriend an engagement ring. For another woman." Claire met Amelia's horror stricken eyes and burst out laughing. It was funny, she knew, she could see it now, just how ridiculous it was, how bizarre and even a little sensational. Amelia was laughing too, which made Claire just laugh harder. "Oh, that felt good," she said, when she'd finally settled down.

"Sounds like you're over him," Amelia observed.

Claire hadn't realized it properly, but strangely, yes, she was. So Matt was getting married; she really didn't even care. Their time together felt so long ago, so different, like it wasn't her present day self but someone else, walking around in a state of resigned bliss, not properly seeing things for what they were.

"Seems like you're over your guy, too," Claire said.

"Well, I can't say that for sure," Amelia gave her a wink. "But, I'm on my way, and that's a start. I'm out of Grey Harbor, I'm moving forward. I'm ready for change.

I want to do something really . . . me, if that makes sense.

Claire nodded. "It makes a lot of sense. Ethan suggested that I start my own shop. Do something with old wedding dresses, maybe vintage accessories."

"I love that idea!" Amelia exclaimed. She shook her head, grinning widely. "Ethan always has good ideas. He sees the world so much more clearly than I do, I suppose."

"That's because he observes it from a distance," Claire said, a little bitterly.

"True," Amelia turned thoughtful. "But he still takes it all in, still takes it to heart. It's just, you, me . . . we dive in with our heart. We can't help it, and that's who we are. But Ethan . . . He's careful. Cautious. Maybe too much so for his own good, but that's what it is really."

Claire nodded, knowing it was true, but it didn't exactly make her feel any better. Since when did Ethan feel the need to protect himself from her?

Since he'd taken the friendship to another level. Or maybe, since he'd started seeing her as more than just a friend.

The realization gave her little comfort. After all, it didn't change a thing. Ethan was still Ethan, keeping love at arm's length. While she . . . Well, she was holding out for more.

Amelia waited until they'd passed the town border to pull into a gas station and stop the car.

"Cigarette break?" Claire teased.

"Jeez, no. I left behind all my vices in Grey Harbor.

Well, except for one. What's a road trip without some junk food?"

Claire laughed and unbuckled her seat belt. It may not be a cure all, but a little chocolate could go a long way for lifting a girl's spirits.

And so, she thought, glancing at Amelia, could a new friend.

*

Ethan sat on an old iron bench under the shade of an overgrown lilac bush, debating whether or not he should go back to the boathouse yet, seek Claire out, or give her time. An hour had passed since she'd left, and he'd given up hope that she'd come back to the party. Luckily, his extended family's interest in his love life had waned now that they were satisfied, and few people had noticed she wasn't by his side for the rest of the brunch. Still, he was struggling to keep up the pretense that everything was fine, exhausted by the strain of pleasantries. He'd made a mess. A big one. And he didn't know how to fix it.

"There you are." Ethan turned at the sound of his mother's voice and saw her coming down the stone path toward the bench where he sat. "If I didn't know better, I might think you were hiding down here."

Ethan's smile felt grim. "That obvious?"

His mother sighed. "It can be exhausting, these long family weekends when everyone is in town. It would be nice if you came home during a quieter time, when there weren't so many distractions."

Ethan nodded. "That would be nice." But somehow, the appeal of coming back to Grey Harbor felt less appealing than it had just a few hours ago. He'd tainted it. Again. Marred it with bad feelings and harsh memories.

"Did Claire go back to the house?" she asked.

Ethan swallowed. Claire was right. They shouldn't have lied to his family, no matter the reason behind it. "Mom, there's something you should know," he said, pulling in a breath. "Claire . . . We're just friends, you see. Good friends."

"She's the same Claire you've talked about for years," his mother commented. She raised an eyebrow. "The name isn't that common, Ethan. I did wonder . . ."

Ethan laughed softly. He hadn't even considered, but of course he'd talked about Claire over the years. No wonder his mother had dared to think it had turned into something more.

"I let you think she was more than a friend so you wouldn't worry, Mom."

"I do worry," his mother sighed. "And I have to say that the past few days I saw a change in you. You were happier than you've been in years."

Ethan looked down at the moss-covered rocks beneath his feet. "I was."

"And now?"

He shook his head. There was no point in stating the obvious. He wasn't happy. In fact, he was downright miserable.

"You know, Ethan, I never said this to you before, but I think it's time now. Don't turn your back to love. Sometimes it doesn't work out, and sometimes it's taken from us. But it doesn't mean it wasn't worth it. Don't shut out the one person you love because you're afraid of what will happen if it doesn't work out."

"But that's just the thing, Mom. I do know what will happen. Claire, that friendship . . . it means everything to me." He dragged a hand down his face. And now that friendship is gone.

"Well, let me ask you this, then. If you could only ever be friends with Claire, would that be enough?"

Ethan frowned. "Yes. No. I don't know anymore."

His mother gave a slow smile. "Then I think that's the answer. Believe in what you have, Ethan. And above all, follow your heart. You might lose her, but at least you'll know you tried. Isn't that better than never knowing?"

Ethan nodded, saying nothing. His mother was right. She was always right. But one thing was certain. He couldn't lose Claire. Not as a friend.

And not, he knew, as something more.

Chapter Twelve

Ethan stood in his silent apartment and stared at his entrance table, his suitcases still at his feet. He knew he should have discarded that answering machine years ago. That, and the habits that went with it. He pressed the flashing button, listening to the voice on the other end confirming their date for tonight. Of course, he thought, cursing under his breath. Another date. He'd set this one up over a week ago with a waitress he met at the gastropub he'd visited again under the pretense of research for his article. He'd struck up a conversation, asked a few questions, and by the end of the night he'd handed her his landline number—he'd learned long ago what happened when he gave out the cellular information—and said something about Sunday. This Sunday. An hour from now, to be exact.

At the time he'd thought it would be a nice distraction from an otherwise tense weekend. A way to immerse himself into his present circumstances and escape the ghosts of the past. And maybe it would be, if the thought of being with a woman other than Claire didn't make him feel agitated and uneasy.

He picked up the phone, and dialed the number back, cringing at the thought of letting the girl down but knowing it was inevitable and, really, better this way. She didn't answer, and he left a message, kind but firm, apologizing for making plans and explaining that he wasn't dating at this time. It was the right thing to do. The fair thing to do.

It was something he should have done a long time ago.

Ethan left his bags in the hall and walked around his empty apartment, the rooms he had chosen not to fill, the walls he had kept high for all but one person. There were no pictures, no frames, no memories here. He'd been careful about that. Except now there was a sense of loss. Of the one person he'd let in, and the one girl he'd shut out.

Claire. He'd been so careful, so determined to preserve what they had, to keep it meaningful, to make it last, and now he'd gone and done the one thing he'd feared the most.

She'd written a note, something about taking a bus back to Chicago. By his estimation she'd be back in town by now. He didn't know if she'd talk to him, and he didn't know what he would say if she ever gave him the chance. Half of him wanted to hail the next cab, knock on her door, tell her he was sorry, and so much more . . .

But it was late. And tonight wasn't a night for impulsive action or shallow escape. For once, he would sit in his apartment, allow himself to think about his past, and maybe even, for once, his future.

No dates. No parties. No more vain attempts to fill the empty part of himself with temporary solutions. It was time to make a change.

*

Claire faced the back of the nubby brown couch and did her best to block the morning sun with her hand, mentally playing Hailey's morning routine, knowing it would only be a matter of minutes, if not less, before the bedroom doorknob turned and her cousin appeared. And then . . . Claire's stomach knotted. Then she'd have to tell her the truth.

The whole truth. There was no way she could hide what had happened over the weekend from Hailey. As much as she wanted to forget any of it had ever happened, it was no use.

She'd planned to blurt it all out last night. Hoped to, really, but Hailey had been out with Lila and Mary for an impromptu Sunday night dinner when she'd arrived home, and she was so worn out, she'd fallen asleep waiting for her. When those three said dinner, they usually meant chatting until the restaurant dimmed its light and turned the sign on the door.

She should have joined them, she thought now. But she wasn't ready to share anything last night. And oh, there would have been questions.

She sat up, wincing at the pain that shot through her lower back, and let out a small whimper of self-pity that she had to sleep on this pull-out, and that it was all her own damn fault. Still, it was motivation, and she was more driven than ever to get things back on track. It would feel so good to have her own space again, a fresh start, and a new outlook. Ethan was right about one thing: a project would keep her busy, take her mind off the heartache. He just hadn't known that when he'd suggested it, the person she'd be trying to put from her mind was him.

Claire blinked away the tears that threatened to spill every time she thought of how empty life already felt. A day had passed without a phone call. They never went so long without talking. The doorknob turned, and Claire's attention was immediately pulled back to the present as Hailey burst into the living room, smiling ear to ear. "Welcome home!"

Home. Yes, that's where she was, but to hear her cousin phrase it that way made her sit up in surprise.

"Coffee?" Hailey was already halfway to the kitchen.

"As if you needed to ask," Claire replied, climbing out of the makeshift bed to fold the mattress back into the sofa frame. It was still early; there was time for this conversation before Hailey left for the café. She had no excuse.

"How was the trip?" Hailey asked as she poured beans into the grinder. Claire didn't dare confess to her cousin that she sort of preferred the instant stuff. It was quick, and it did the job. But Hailey took her coffee very seriously. Only ordered certain beans. Ground them herself. She could only imagine her cousin's reaction if she knew Claire couldn't really taste much difference for all that trouble . . .

"Oh, fine. Fine. Not much to tell." Claire managed a smile, but it felt forced.

Sure enough, Hailey looked at her sharply. "Fine? Just fine?" She stopped grinding the beans. "What happened?"

"Nothing. Really. It was just a wedding. Low key. Home now . . ." Claire inspected a fingernail. The nail polish she'd applied the morning she'd left for the trip was already chipping.

"If nothing happened, then why won't you look me in the eyes? And why'd you ignore every one of my calls, too?" Hailey started and then, with a pop of her eyes, held a finger in the air and all but screamed, "You slept with him!"

Claire was frantically biting her nail by now, and she couldn't even deny the truth. It was no use. Hailey knew her too well.

"I am going to finish making this coffee, and then you and I are going to sit. And chat. And you, my dear, are going to tell me everything."

"Don't you have to go to work?" Claire asked hopefully.

"Summer staff," Hailey explained. "I love seasonal help. I don't need to be there until noon today. And you have some time before work, right? Now go. Sit."

It was an order, and Claire slumped her shoulders and marched back into the living room, where she dropped down onto the couch and waited for the coffee to finish, the minutes ticking by as the smell of roasted beans filled the air.

Finally, Hailey appeared through the doorway with a tray, her mouth set in a determined line, her stride purposeful and quick.

"So," she said, after she had deposited the tray on the coffee table and distractedly sloshed some cream into her mug. She eyed Claire carefully. "You and Ethan slept together. No surprise, of course."

"*No surprise?*" Claire choked on her coffee. When she'd finished coughing, she set down her mug and gave her cousin a long look. "What does that mean?"

Hailey curled up into the air chair, tucking her feet under her as she clutched her oversized mug bearing the little "H." "Come on, Claire. You can't tell me you're surprised either. You and Ethan have been dancing around this for years."

"We have not!" Claire protested, but she blinked, trying to process this accusation. Had they?

Hailey just tipped her chin and gave her a long look. Okay, so maybe they had.

"Ethan's hot. Like, really hot. And before you go arguing with me, can we just agree that this is an indisputable fact?" Hailey sipped her coffee.

Claire felt like she could suddenly cry again as his handsome image swam to the forefront of her mind. If she closed her eyes, she could picture his face, so close to hers, just before he kissed her. See the wide grin on his face as he chased her up the stairs to his bedroom. The anguish in his eyes the last time they'd spoke.

"Wow." Hailey set her mug down, giving Claire her full attention. "You've got it bad. You like him. You . . . love him!"

"Well, of course I love him," Claire said hastily. "He's my best friend. He's like the male version of you."

Hailey laughed. "Nice try, but no. I'm your cousin. And Ethan . . . Well, Ethan is his own special beast."

"It doesn't matter," Claire said. "He can't commit."

"Just because he hasn't before doesn't mean he can't now."

Claire shook her head adamantly, hating the thread of hope she heard in that statement. "No. He has committed. To someone else. And I don't think he ever got over her. I'm just his friend. That's all it could ever be."

His friend, and the rebound girl, she thought bitterly.

"Maybe so, but what you and Ethan have is special. Are you really telling me you can't still be friends?"

Claire looked blearily out the window onto the tree-lined street. "I don't see how. That's the worst part of it, honestly."

"Oh, honey." Hailey came over and settled herself on the couch. "You know one good thing came from this, though, right? At least you're over Matt."

Despite herself, Claire laughed, but then all at once burst into tears. She'd thought losing Matt was hard, but Ethan . . . it was so much worse. There was so much there. So much more to lose.

"Speaking of Matt . . ." Claire dragged out a long sigh. She couldn't keep up the pretense anymore.

The doorbell rang, interrupting her well-rehearsed speech, and Hailey's quizzical expression matched her own. Claire checked her watch. It wasn't even eight. Who could be here at this hour?

Her heart thudded. Ethan.

"Go," Hailey whispered, giving her a little push. "Go."

Claire smoothed her hair and walked slowly to the door, her chest pounding as she considered what there even was to say.

She took the stairs slowly, stopping only once to clutch the banister and collect herself, reminding herself that this was Ethan. Her best friend. But somehow he wasn't anymore. In less than a day he'd morphed from being her source of comfort and happiness into someone who had the potential to play with her emotions and break her heart.

The realization that this could be their last conversation cut her deep, but as much as she wanted to avoid him, close her ears to the words he might say, another part of her was hopping with excitement at the prospect of seeing him again. It was always that way. She never tired of him.

She groaned to herself. Why hadn't she seen it before? She'd been in love with Ethan for years. She just hadn't stopped to admit it before.

She wrapped her hand around the doorknob, counted to three, and opened it.

"Amelia!" Claire blinked at Ethan's sister, feeling her confusion grow. She skirted her eyes down the street, but there was no one else around aside from an elderly woman with a penchant for sweeping the sidewalk outside her brownstone. "What are you doing here? Did you lose something? Did I accidentally take something from the car when I got my luggage?"

For one hopeful moment she thought maybe Ethan had sent her, that she was here to try to lure Claire down to the West Loop, host an intervention of sorts that would make everything right, or maybe everything the way it used to be. If such a thing were possible.

"I was thinking about what you said last night in the car. About that vintage bridal shop." Amelia slurped coffee from the plastic lid of her paper cup. Her eyes were hidden behind sunglasses. In her cut-off shorts and tank top, she looked younger somehow, even though she was older than Claire by five years. Refreshed, Claire thought. Amelia was a new woman. Overnight, she had been transformed.

It was almost . . . inspiring.

"Well, it was just an idea," Claire stammered. "More of a pipe dream really."

Amelia tipped her head. "How so?"

"Well, a new business costs money," Claire pointed out, suddenly feeling a little impatient. She glanced back up the stairs, hoping that Hailey wasn't able to overhear any part of this conversation. She needed to stop fantasizing about things that couldn't realistically happen and start cleaning up her mess. It started with telling Hailey the truth. After, she needed to find a job. Strike that, she needed to *reclaim* her life. Amelia style.

"I have money," Amelia said flatly.

Claire felt her eyes pop. "What? No. No." She was shaking her head frantically. "I hadn't meant to ask. I mean, I wasn't hinting . . . I mean, it was a good idea, but I'm looking for a real job. Well, a paying job. So . . . maybe someday." Yes, someday. Someday she might have that little shop.

"I know you weren't asking." Claire could almost detect Amelia's eye roll through her shades. "I'm offering. You have a good idea and I need a job. A job I enjoy, something that will keep me very busy. Plus, I'm a whizz on a sewing machine."

"Really?" Claire could only stare at the woman standing before her, wondering if this was really happening.

"You know those bridesmaids dresses? I made them."

"You—" Now this was entirely too much. "I guess I just thought . . ."

"That I hated weddings because I was so depressed to be single?" Amelia grinned. "Well, yeah, sort of, but I like to sew. It relaxes me." She lifted her sunglasses onto her forehead and looked Claire straight in the eye. "So what do you say? Partners?"

Claire could think of a hundred reasons to say no, or at least that she needed some time to think about it, but no matter how many times her heart had been broken or her path had been altered, when something irresistible came along, she wasn't afraid to recognize it.

*

Claire tied her apron strings tighter on her waist and began foaming the milk for a cappuccino. She was getting better at it; no doubt she'd be an expert by the time she stopped pulling shifts here. If she ever stopped pulling shifts, she thought.

Hailey was kind enough to give her some hours that very afternoon, as if she'd ever doubted her cousin would come through for her, and Claire was grateful for the work. And the chance to keep busy. Even though she'd only been back in Chicago for a day, something was missing. It was with her, weighing heavily, even as she cheerfully took the orders from the customers who lined up at Corner Beanery for their afternoon pick-me-up.

Claire brightened as Lila pushed through the door and beelined for the counter. Claire checked her watch, and despite the heaviness in her heart, grinned at her friend. "I expected you here an hour ago," she quipped, referring to Lila's three-o'clock coffee habit. With her advertising agency just down Armitage Avenue in a charming walk-up brownstone, it was easy for Lila to pop in and out of the café when she needed a break. Claire and Hailey always looked forward to her visits, but today, Claire was especially pleased by it.

"Long meeting." Lila leaned in to the counter as Claire started preparing the next order. "You don't have to work at the jewelry store today?"

"Oh." Claire skirted her eyes. "That didn't work out."

"Better to know that now," Lila remarked. She grinned. "It just means something better is waiting for you."

Claire warmed a little at that thought. It was true, she supposed, that when one opportunity ended, it left the door open for something else.

"How was the weekend up in Door County?"

Claire did her best to keep her expression neutral. In time she'd tell Lila and her sister Mary what had transpired up there, but for today, she needed to forget it. As if that were possible, she thought, feeling her lips thin.

She kept her eyes trained on the machine as she emptied the shot of espresso into a paper cup and added the hot milk. "It's pretty up there."

"You know Ethan's a nice guy. I've always liked him. A little misunderstood, if you ask me, though."

Claire tried not to react when her heart skipped a beat. "Oh?" She kept her tone neutral and light, but it was no use. She could see the glint in Lila's eyes.

"Oh, you know, he's all about partying, having a good time, never settling down. But you know what they say…"

Claire's smile felt shaky. "No. What do they say?"

"He who doth protest too much . . ." Lila winked. "Okay, I'm off to place my order. I've been dreaming about a double-chocolate chip muffin for two hours."

Claire grinned a little easier. "One of those days?"

"Monday. I've officially reached the point where I'll be happy to have this wedding behind me. Too many last minute details to worry about on top of too many demanding clients. Let's just hope the week gets better from here."

One can hope, Claire thought as she watched her friend walk over to talk to Hailey who was setting out a fresh tray of baked goods at the end of the display case.

The café was jumping this afternoon, Claire noted, and even with the extra seasonal help, she could see that she was needed. Hailey whipped together extra cookies and scones in the kitchen while one of the newer girls manned the counter and Claire worked the espresso machine. She called out order after order, enjoying the pace of it, barely stopping to brush the hair that slipped from her ponytail as the machine hissed and steamed.

"Double Americano!" she called out, not bothering to notice the hand that reached for the paper cup.

"Thanks," a familiar voice said, and Claire startled, burning her wrist on the contraption, as she looked up to see Ethan. He was smiling at her, but there was uncertainty in his eyes, and for a moment, neither of them said anything.

"I see you came clean to Hailey," he said, motioning to her apron.

"First thing this morning." She nodded curtly, hating the clipped tone of her voice. She was being defensive, pushing him away, when all part of her wanted to do was reach out and grab him, go back to the way things used to be.

She looked down at her wrist, noticing the red welt that was starting to form. They could never go back to the way things used to be. As much as she wished they could, too much had happened.

"Ouch." Ethan winced and reached out to touch her wrist.

Claire pulled it away before he could touch her again. "It's fine," she insisted.

"No, it's not fine," he said firmly. "You should put some ice on it. Come on, let's go back to the kitchen."

She searched his face, trying to keep the emotions from creeping into her voice. "Why are you doing this?"

"Because I care," he said simply.

She swallowed hard, squeezed her aching wrist. "I

want to believe that," she said softly. "But—"

"Claire!" Claire turned to see Hailey staring at her aghast, her eyes darting from Ethan to her and back again. Her gaze dropped to Claire's wrist and she leaned in to study it, pulling at Claire's elbow while asking one of the new girls to fill the coffee orders.

"He's here, Hailey," Claire hissed as they pushed through the door to the kitchen. "What's he doing here?"

"I don't know," Hailey said, marching over to the freezer to retrieve an ice pack. She handed it to her. "But I suggest you hear him out." She slid her eyes to the door, where Ethan was standing, still holding the Americano Claire had made for him.

"Why aren't you at work?" she asked when Hailey went back into the storefront. "It's only four o'clock."

"Research." He grinned. "I met with my boss this morning. The party scene was fun, but I'm ready for something new. You're looking at the new face of Chicago's culture scene."

Claire hated the smile that was quirking the corner of her mouth. It was too easy with Ethan. Too tempting to fall back onto old ways.

"Culture?" She looked at him doubtfully. "Like plays and museums?"

"And coffee shops," he said. He sighed and set the drink down. "Okay, not coffee shops. I'm here because I couldn't wait, Claire. I didn't like how we left things off yesterday."

"Neither did I," she admitted, feeling her thick voice

betraying her. "I miss our friendship. I suppose I always will. But I don't think we can go back to the way things were."

"Me either," he said, catching her by surprise.

Claire pinched her lips, her anger making her forget all about the throbbing pain shooting up to her elbow. "Well, then why are you here?"

"To tell you I don't want to be your friend, Claire. Maybe I never did. I just didn't dare to try for more. Until this weekend." He took a step toward her, and her heart began to pound, trying to understand what he was saying.

"But Kimberly."

Ethan brushed a hand through the air. "Kimberly hurt me. I won't deny that. But my feelings for her were more about the loss than the hope of getting back together. For the record, I didn't sleep with you to take my mind off her. I wanted to be with you, Claire. I still do."

"Ethan." Claire shook her head, trying to make sense of this. "You're my best friend."

"And you're mine," he said, reaching down to take her hands, ice pack and all.

"And what if it doesn't work out?" The pain of the last two days was still with her. "I don't know if I can go through the feeling of losing you again."

"Maybe we never have to. But we won't know unless we try." He pushed the ice pack onto her wrist, holding it there, and then looked deep into her eyes. "I don't know what will happen to us, Claire. All I know is that I love you. I've always loved you. And I can't walk out that door without making sure you know it, and that I've tried."

Claire stopped blinking back her tears now and instead let them fall. She didn't bother to fight him when he set his hands around her waist and pulled her close. He felt warm and familiar and like where she was supposed to be. Where she wanted to be.

"Promise me nothing will change?" she asked, looking up into his eyes.

He tucked a strand of hair behind her hair and leaned down to kiss her mouth. "Oh things will change, honey. But only for the better. Only for the better."

Epilogue

"I still can't believe you're going into business with Amelia," Ethan marveled as he looked around the empty storefront that would soon be transformed into something magical enough to make Claire giddy with excitement.

It was hard to believe they were opening in a week. There was still so much to do: the dressing rooms needed to be finished, the three-way vintage mirrors set up, and there were still at least two dozen sample veils to be sewn. Still, in the three months since she and Amelia had first sat down and brainstormed, a lot had been accomplished. Claire felt the urge to pinch herself. It really was almost too good to be true.

"Is it so hard to believe?" Claire asked, as she popped the lid on a can of creamy, pale blue paint that would cover the walls of Something Borrowed. She and Amelia had come up with the name of the store during one of their many weekly meetings, deciding that Something Old just didn't send the same message, even if it might be a bit more accurate.

"No, well, yes." Ethan grinned. "Who knows, maybe you guys will expand and open a second shop in Grey Harbor."

"Don't get ahead of yourself there," Claire said, setting a hand on his chest as she pushed past him to the big bay window where she imagined three mannequins showing off their latest collection. "But stranger things have happened," she said, turning over her shoulder to give him a slow grin.

Amelia came in through the back office, sneezing at the dust. "I'm afraid I can't stay late tonight, if that's all right."

Claire looked at her with interest. "Another date with the mystery man?"

Amelia blushed and tried to busy herself by counting satin padded clothes hangers, even though they'd just counted them this morning, and knew there to be exactly ten dozen.

"When are you going to tell us his name?" Ethan asked. He brushed a strip of paint near the window frame and lifted an eyebrow at Claire for approval.

Claire nodded. It was perfect. Like everything else about the store, thus far. Oh, she knew that it wouldn't always be an easy road, but then, nothing in life was. And sometimes, the best things were the ones worth fighting for. She looked at Ethan, feeling her heart melt just a little.

"It's still new," Amelia huffed impatiently. "I don't want to get ahead of myself."

Claire and Ethan exchanged secret smiles as she stood to help him edge the wall. A lot had changed in three months. And all for the better, so far. Amelia was dating, and taking it slow, not going all in at once like she had in that past. Ethan's cultural column was even a bigger success than the social beat, and there was talk of him being up for assistant editor by the year end . . . right around the time their new condo would be ready for occupancy. As much as Claire knew Hailey would appreciate having her apartment to herself again, both girls would secretly miss being roommates. Something told Claire they might never have the chance again.

"Well, I'm off," Amelia said, setting the hangers to the side and slinging her oversized handbag over a shoulder.

"Have fun!" Claire called out.

"Don't do anything I wouldn't do," warned Ethan jovially.

Amelia stopped at the door and nailed her brother with a hard look. "Which would basically mean everything, at this point. You've turned into pretty much the least exciting guy there is."

"Hey, there's nothing boring about being happy," he said wisely, and Amelia just rolled her eyes and pushed into the door with her hip, but she was smiling as she walked past the window a moment later, her arm held high to hail a passing a cab.

"So you're happy then, are you?" Claire asked, keeping her eyes fixed on the wall and the pretty blue paint that was slowly transforming the space, making it her own.

"Never thought it would happen, did you?" Ethan stopped painting long enough for her to turn and look at him properly.

He already had a streak of paint on his cheek and another above his eyebrow, but Claire didn't bother to point it out. This was exactly how she wanted to always think of him, at her side, supporting her dreams, not afraid to get a little dirty doing it. "You and me? Never thought it possible, honestly."

Ethan set his brush down and wrapped his arms around her waist and pulled her in for a kiss. "Anything is possible, honey. Haven't you figured that out yet?"

Olivia Miles is a bestselling author of contemporary romance. A city girl with a fondness for small town charm, Olivia enjoys highlighting both ways of life in her stories. She currently resides just outside Chicago with her husband, daughter, and two ridiculously pampered pups.

Olivia loves connecting with readers. Please visit her website at www.OliviaMilcsBooks.com to learn more.